QUEEN
FOR A DAY

Also by Barbara Cohen

Benny
The Binding of Isaac
Bitter Herbs and Honey
The Carp in the Bathtub
I Am Joseph
The Innkeeper's Daughter
R My Name Is Rosie
Thank You, Jackie Robinson
Where's Florrie?

QUEEN
FOR A DAY
Barbara Cohen

Lothrop, Lee & Shepard Books
New York

Printed in the United States of America.
First Edition
1 2 3 4 5 6 7 8 9 10

Library of Congress Cataloging in Publication Data
Cohen, Barbara.
   Queen for a day.
   SUMMARY: Twelve-year-old Gertie's difficult life
with her stern grandmother and two selfish, young
aunts is eased when a new boarder comes to stay.
   [1. Jews in the United States—Fiction] I. Title.
PZ7.C6595Qe   [Fic]   80-28115
ISBN 0-688-00437-7
ISBN 0-688-00438-5 (lib. bdg.)

In memory of my grandmother
Anne Brookner Marshall

ONE

Every morning I got up at six. No one woke me, and I had no alarm clock. I just got up at six because I knew I had to. If I didn't bring back hot rolls for breakfast before quarter of seven, one of the aunts might hit me. Aunt Lilly especially had a temper. She'd already slapped me once or twice. The memory was enough to make me wake up exactly on time each morning.

I liked walking down Pitkin Avenue in the pink summer dawn. It was one of the busiest streets in all of Brooklyn, and I wasn't the only person out on it first thing in the morning. I would wave to Mr. Goldfarb, the milkman, and sometimes he let me pet his horse. The milk company said the horse's name was Dobbin, but Mr. Goldfarb called him Shlepperman. On my way home, I'd pass Mr. Rinaldi, the iceman, and if the morning was already warm, he'd give me a piece of ice to suck. I knew all the early morning people.

But in the winter, or if it was raining, the trip to the bakery wasn't much fun. I'd run all the way in order to be sure the rolls—and I—were still warm by the time we got home. Sometimes I'd slip on the ice and tear my long black stockings. One miserable January day, I accidentally splashed in a puddle and walked back into our flat with mud on my high-top shoes and my navy-blue serge skirt.

"Look, Mama," Aunt Lilly said, "Gertie's gotten her skirt all dirty. It's the one I gave her too. I'm not going to give her any more of my clothes if that's the way she's going to treat them."

"Well, her shoes used to be mine," Aunt Berenice put in her two cents. "The skirt you can clean, but the shoes are really ruined."

"Oh, shut up, both of you," I burst out. "These

clothes don't fit you anyway. What do you care what happens to them?"

"Mama!" Aunt Lilly screamed. "She's talking fresh again. Make her stop."

But she didn't slap me. She couldn't when Grandma was there. All Grandma did was look at me and say, "You're a mess, Gertie. Put breakfast on the table and then change before you go to school. You'll have to wear your dress. Don't forget to rinse out what you take off before you leave. While you're at it, you can wash the other things in the laundry tub too."

No breakfast for me again. Well, there'd be a roll left that I could eat on my way to school. I wasn't going to say anything about missing breakfast, because then Grandma would just tell me to eat it after I did the laundry and forget about going to school. She wanted me to quit anyway. Lilly and Berenice were fourteen and fifteen, and they were going to quit high school at the end of the term and go to work in garment factories and make six dollars a week. Soon I'd be thirteen. Grandma said I should quit too, and earn my keep by helping around the house until I was old enough to go out to work.

"I do help around the house," I protested every time she brought the matter up.

"Not enough," she said.

"I do whatever you tell me," I reminded her.

"Well, what can I tell you to do when you're at school?" she asked. "Lilly and Berenice are quitting."

"They want to quit. I don't. I like school."

"School is a waste of time for an orphan like you, Gertie," Grandma said.

I blinked my eyes hard so I wouldn't cry. "I'm not an orphan. I have a mother and a father."

"Yes," she replied, "a mother in a lunatic asylum that she'll never come out of, and a father out West somewhere, 'making his fortune.' I'll be pushing up the daisies, and so will you, before we see hide or hair of him or his fortune."

Aunt Lilly, Aunt Berenice, and Grandma sat down at the kitchen table to eat the rolls and drink coffee. I took off my skirt, carried it to the washtub in the corner of the kitchen, and stood there in my middy blouse and petticoat, rinsing it in cold water. Though the day was chilly and damp, I wasn't shivering. Grandma made all three of us wear long underwear until April 1.

It wasn't actually raining, so after I had done the washing, I took off my blouse, put on my good dress and my coat, and carried the laundry outside to the little square of backyard where each tenant in the building had a piece of clothesline. I hung the laundry on the line, threw the basket back into the rear entryway, and ran all the way to school.

But even so I was late. The schoolyard was empty when I arrived. I ran up the steps, through the front door, down the corridor, and into my classroom. Miss Needham had her back to the students; she was writing the spelling lesson on the board. I slipped quietly into my seat in the second row from the rear. Perhaps she wouldn't notice that I'd come in late. Or rather, perhaps she would pretend not to notice. Nothing escaped Miss Needham, not even when her back was turned. But she liked me. She wouldn't punish me if she could get away with it.

No such luck, not with Fanny Mercer sitting in the front of the room. When Miss Needham turned to face the class, Fanny's hand shot up like an arrow.

Miss Needham, her face grim, nodded at Fanny.

"Miss Needham, Gertie was late again," Fanny announced, her tone triumphant.

Miss Needham's face was still grim as she nodded at Fanny once again. Then she looked at me. "You'll have to stay after school for an hour, Gertie."

"Yes, ma'am," I replied. That meant I'd never get

the kitchen floor scrubbed before it was time to start supper. Grandma would be hopping mad and would start in on me again about quitting school. But so far as staying after itself was concerned, I didn't mind. I'd never admit such a thing out loud, but it was the truth.

"Just an hour, Miss Needham?" Fanny murmured. "This is the second time she's been late this week."

The face Miss Needham now turned on Fanny was more than grim. It was positively stony. "Tattling is the least attractive of all possible human behavior. Please try to remember that, Fanny."

Ellen O'Grady giggled and Miss Needham turned next to her. "The second least attractive behavior," she continued coldly, "is giggling." Ellen shut up, and so, of course, did Fanny, though if looks could kill, I'd have died on the spot. Fortunately they couldn't, and I was used to Fanny anyway. When I had entered the school in the middle of sixth grade, she was teacher's pet. I soon understood that she had always been teacher's pet. She couldn't accept the fact that in the seventh grade I'd displaced her. But to tell the truth, I don't think she'd have been Miss Needham's pet even if I hadn't been there. Fanny wasn't Miss Needham's type, and Miss Needham wasn't Fanny's.

In spite of the chill, during recess Ellen and I went outside to eat our lunches on the front steps of the school building. It was better than hanging around the stuffy classroom, smelling other people's onions and sardines. We had barely removed our bread and margarine from its waxed-paper wrapping when Fanny and her two cronies, Ethel Baum and Maggie Pryce, came out of the front door. "This is our place," Fanny said. "We always eat here."

"So do we," Ellen said. "You haven't been outside for lunch in three months."

"But we're out here today," Ethel snapped, "and we don't want to eat on the same steps with you."

"Why not?" Ellen asked. "There's plenty of room. They're not your steps."

"We don't eat with hired help," Fanny announced grandly.

"Well, who's hired help?" Ellen wanted to know. I wished with all my heart that Ellen would shut her mouth. She was playing right into their hands.

Fanny didn't deign to reply, but merely pointed her finger at me. I said nothing. I knew what Fanny was talking about.

"She is not," Ellen defended me staunchly. "She's the smartest girl in the class."

"Her mother is crazy," Fanny said. "Her father ran off. Her grandmother only keeps her because she scrubs the floor and does the laundry."

Silently I collected my lunch things, stood up, and walked away. Ellen ran after me. She grabbed my arm and shook it. "Are you going to let her get away with that?" she asked furiously. "It's a free country. Anyone can sit on those steps who wants to."

"I don't want to sit with her," I said, "any more than she wants to sit with me. But you can stay with her if you want. I don't care."

"Well, I don't want to either," Ellen said. "I'm coming with you."

"Ellen . . ."

She caught the sober note in my voice. "What is it, Gertie?"

"Who told Fanny about all the work I have to do?"

Ellen's eyes looked away from me and down at her feet.

"You're the only person who knew," I went on. "You're the only one in this school I ever told." It was bad enough everyone in the neighborhood gossiped about my mother and father. Neither Berenice nor Lilly found it necessary to keep family secrets like that to themselves. But they'd never tell anyone about all the work I had to do, because they didn't think I did so much, and I'd never told anyone about it either, except Ellen, once, like a fool.

"Look, Gertie," Ellen said, the words rushing out of her mouth in a breathless torrent, "I was trying to explain to Fanny and the others so they'd leave you alone, so I was telling them how hard you have to work, because your mother's sick and your father's off making his fortune, and no one gives your grandmother any money for you, so you have to earn your keep by helping, and that's why you're late to school sometimes."

"I didn't give you leave to tell them," I said. I was really angry. "I don't have to explain myself to anybody."

"I'm sorry, Gertie, I really am," Ellen apologized. "I thought I was doing you a favor. I feel terrible that you don't see it that way."

"Forget it, Ellen. It's all right." I started down the walk toward the opening in the fence that surrounded the schoolyard. Ellen refused to leave my side. She stretched her short legs to keep up with me. I was twice as tall as she and could cover a lot of ground quickly. Without breaking my stride, I said to her, "I'll just never tell you anything again. Never."

That got her. She stopped moving. She stood stock-still on the pavement. I went right on, down to the fence, out the gate, and around the block. I walked around the block twice. When I got back, recess was ending. I ran into the building, trailing behind the others, and took my seat without speaking to Ellen again, without even looking at her. I didn't need Ellen. Mr. Goldfarb, the milkman, and Mr. Rinaldi, the iceman, would have to be friends enough for me.

I was the only student who had to stay after school that day. Miss Needham had me wash the boards. She didn't talk to me while I was working. When I was done, there were still fifteen minutes left to my hour. Miss Needham told me to sit down in the seat right in front of her desk. Then she sat in her own chair. "Perhaps, Gertie," she began, "you could get up a little earlier in the morning so that you could get to school on time. You're a very good student. It's silly for you to have to stay after school for an hour once or twice a week instead of just getting up five minutes sooner each morning." Her voice was quiet and reasonable, without its usual sharp, ironic tone.

"I have a lot to do before I leave for school," I explained. "Sometimes things come up, unexpectedly."

"Like what, Gertie?"

"Just things." I wasn't going to tell her all that I'd

once told Ellen. How did I know Miss Needham wouldn't blabble all over the school too?

"Perhaps I ought to speak to your grandmother," she suggested.

"No!" I cried hastily. "Please don't do that."

"Why, Gertie? I won't complain about you. I have nothing except your tardiness to complain about. I'll start by telling her what a good student you are and how much I admire your work."

"She knows that. She's seen my report card."

"But perhaps the words coming right from your teacher's mouth will mean more to her than some pen trackings on a piece of cardboard. And then I'll ask ask her if she can find ways to help you get to school on time."

I had to say something. I had to convince Miss Needham to stay away from my grandmother. I decided to tell her part of the truth, without too many details. "Look," I said, "my grandmother doesn't believe in too much education, and she doesn't have much money. She wants me to quit school and help around the house until I can go to work. So if you tell her that you don't like my coming late, she'll just tell me not to come at all."

"This is 1913, not 1813." Miss Needham's voice was

sharp and angry again. "There's a law against that."

"A law?"

"A law that says children must stay in school until they're fourteen," she explained.

I shrugged. Miss Needham knew even better than I that hundreds of students quit school before they were fourteen every week of the year. No one did much of anything about it if they weren't too young, and if they were immigrants' children, like me.

Miss Needham glanced at the clock. There were still five minutes left to my hour. "You can go now, Gertie," she said. "Thank you for washing the boards."

"You're very welcome," I told her. "I'll do them any time, even if I don't have to stay after school. You won't speak to my grandmother, will you?"

"Maybe you underestimate your grandmother," she replied. "But I won't speak to her if you're so set against it." She didn't sound too happy about saying that. I could only hope that she would keep her word.

I stood up. She reached inside one of her desk drawers and pulled out a book. "Perhaps you'd like to borrow this. It's enjoyable reading." That was the main reason I didn't mind staying after school. She often lent me books when no one else was around.

"Thank you," I said. I took the book and glanced

at the title. It was an odd one—*Daddy Long Legs*. Could a book about a bug be described as enjoyable reading? I smiled and pressed it close to me. I would start it that very evening. I read late at night, after all my housework and homework were done. Usually everyone else was asleep. It was the only time I had. I couldn't read in my bedroom because I shared it with Lilly and Berenice, and the light would disturb them. So I read in the kitchen, and if Grandma got up to go to the bathroom and caught me, she sent me to bed. "What are you doing, burning a light at this hour?" she'd say. "You think I'm a millionaire? Get some rest, before you get sick. That's all I need, you to get sick." But I'd rather read than sleep, so the next night I'd sneak out again, hoping she wouldn't wake up this time. Because I was so often interrupted, it sometimes took me a long while to get through a book.

"I'll get this back to you as soon as I can," I said to Miss Needham.

"No hurry," she replied. "Take your time."

"Thanks," I said again.

"Good night, Gertie."

"Good night, Miss Needham."

I hurried back to my own desk, grabbed my schoolbooks, retrieved my coat from the cloakroom, left the building, and walked the twelve long blocks home as quickly as I could. Grandma would be mad that I was late. Before I could settle down with *Daddy Long Legs* there were hours and hours to get through, and piles and piles of things to do.

TWO

But Grandma didn't yell at me when I got home. She was sitting in the parlor, which was also her bedroom, with a strange man, and when she heard me come through the door, she called to me.

"Gertie," she said. "Come meet Mr. Neufeld. He's our new boarder. Mr. Neufeld, this is my granddaughter, Gertie Warshefsky. She lives here too."

"How do you do, Mr. Neufeld?" I said politely. I knew how important a boarder was to Grandma. Grandma talked about how poor she was all the time. All she had was the insurance money that Lilly and

Berenice's father had left her and the rent a boarder paid. Of course, there was always enough to eat in her house, and no one walked around in rags. But she'd been very upset when Mrs. Ackerman had left, and the little room where Mrs. Ackerman had stayed had been empty now for two weeks. Grandma must have been desperate to take in a man. However, male boarders were easier to find than women.

And Mr. Neufeld certainly appeared harmless enough. He was a short, thin man with wisps of gray hair plastered across the bald spot on his head. He wore gold-rimmed eyeglasses, from behind which large, soft brown eyes peered intently, and he had a little gray mustache beneath his big, bumpy nose.

Mr. Neufeld got up from his chair and bowed slightly from the waist. "Good afternoon, Miss Warshefsky," he said. No one had ever called me *Miss* Warshefsky before. "I hope my taking up residence here won't inconvenience you in any way," he continued. His Yiddish accent was heavy, heavier than Grandma's, but he used beautiful words.

Grandma glared at me and I found my tongue. "Oh, of course not, Mr. Neufeld," I mumbled. "We're very glad to have you."

"Put clean sheets on Mr. Neufeld's bed," Grandma instructed.

"I did, Grandma," I replied. "I scrubbed the whole room from top to bottom after Mrs. Ackerman left, remember?"

"Well, be sure to dust it before you start on the kitchen."

I nodded. It was lucky I had changed the linen after Mrs. Ackerman left. We didn't have an extra set of bed sheets. I took them off the beds early on fine Monday mornings, washed them, hung them out to dry, and put them back on the beds before we went to sleep.

I went into the room I shared with Aunt Lilly and Aunt Berenice. They weren't home yet. I put my schoolbooks on the shelf above my canvas cot. Lilly and Berenice slept in a double bed. They had a dresser too, for their clothes, while my things were folded on a shelf. That didn't matter, though, because I didn't have much.

I took off my good dress and put on my middy and skirt. The skirt was dry now, and Grandma had brought it in from the line along with the rest of the laundry I'd done that morning. When I went back into the parlor, Mr. Neufeld was gone. Grandma said he'd left to get this things, but would be back for dinner. I dusted his bedroom, scrubbed the kitchen floor, and started on the ironing. Grandma got supper. Mostly, she didn't trust me with the cooking. Sometimes, though, Berenice made things to eat. She was fairly good at it. I liked her noodle pudding and her tsimmes. Lilly was good only at looking pretty. Between curling her hair with a curling iron and trying on four different shirtwaists before she was satisfied, it took her an hour to get dressed each morning.

I was ironing one of Lilly's waists when she came home. It was nearly five-thirty. "So where you been all this time?" Grandma asked her. "School lets out at three."

"Oh, just walking," Lilly said with an airy wave of her hand. "The soup smells good, Mama."

"Don't change the subject, Lilly," Grandma said. "Walking with who?"

"Morrie Weissbinder," Lilly admitted.

"I told you, watch out for him," Grandma scolded. "I told you I don't trust him."

"Why not, Mama?" Lilly whined. "He's so smart. He says he's going to be a lawyer."

"So that's what I mean," Grandma said. "He has to

finish high school. Then he wants to go to college. Then he has to read law. What are you going to do? Wait for him all those years and then watch him marry some rich German from Riverside Drive?"

"Mama, sometimes you talk so silly. I'm not marrying Morrie, and he's not marrying me. We just took a walk."

"So that's what I mean," Grandma repeated darkly. "You're old enough to start thinking about your future."

"I think about it all the time." Lilly opened the bread drawer, took out a roll left over from breakfast, and began to eat it.

"You'll spoil your supper," Grandma said.

"I'm hungry enough to eat two suppers." Lilly did eat a lot, and she never put on an ounce of weight.

"The least that Weissbinder boy could have done was buy you a hot chocolate."

"Oh, Mama," Lilly protested, "he's saving all his money for school. You know that." She wandered toward the ironing board and ran her hand over her shirtwaist. "Be careful of that, Gertie," she warned. "It's my best one. Don't burn it."

"I haven't burned a waist yet," I reminded her. "I'm not planning to start in now, Lilly."

27

"*Aunt* Lilly to you, Miss Fresh," she retorted. She and Berenice had insisted on that "Aunt" since I'd first learned to talk.

I felt like burning the waist on purpose, but I didn't. I would have had not only Lilly down on me for that, but Grandma too, on account of the expense.

Berenice came in a few minutes later. After school she helped Mrs. Wagner, a dressmaker over on Pitkin Avenue. Mrs. Wagner gave Berenice a quarter each day, and Berenice said she was learning a lot besides. But she didn't like Mrs. Wagner and she was planning to quit as soon as she knew all that Mrs. Wagner could teach her.

"Boy, I'm starved," Berenice said as she dropped her books on the kitchen cupboard. "You'd think that old skinflint could give me a cup of tea when I got there. She knows I haven't had a bite since lunch. A cup of tea and a crust of bread. That's all I ask. And she's got plenty of money. I know it. You should see the stuff she has in her china closet."

"Save some of your lunch for after school," Grandma suggested.

"But I'm always hungry at lunchtime," Berenice groaned. "No matter how much I bring, I always eat it up right away." Unlike Lilly, Berenice tended to put on weight. "Let's have dinner right this minute."

"We got to wait for our new boarder," Grandma said. "Set the table."

"Oh, I'm too tired," Berenice protested, sinking into Grandma's rocker. "I worked all afternoon. Let Gertie do it. She's almost through with the ironing." Lilly, seeing what was coming, had, as usual, conveniently disappeared.

"Set the table, Gertie," Grandma commanded. "Berenice worked all afternoon."

"What do you think I did?" I retorted.

Grandma turned away from the stove and stared at me. "I'm not one of your aunts," she said, her voice slow and dark. "I'm your grandma. One more fresh remark and you're in that orphanage, where you belong."

"I'm sorry, Grandma," I murmured. I wasn't, not really, but what could I do? I didn't want to go into the orphanage, like Sadie Weil and her little brother. After their mother had died, their father had put them away like that and they'd just disappeared, as if they didn't exist anymore. Their father had disappeared too, but I didn't care about him. I cared about Sadie. She'd been a good friend when I'd lived with my parents in the old neighborhood, and then she was gone and I never saw her again. The orphanage swallowed her up.

Grandma went back to her cooking. I finished the waist, laid it on top of the rest of the ironing in the basket, put the flatirons on the back of the stove to cool, folded away the ironing board, and started setting the table. Then Mr. Neufeld came in, carrying two suitcases and a basket. "I hired a cart to bring my books over tomorrow," he said. "I've got two boxes full, and they're too heavy to carry."

Grandma was all smiles now. "Just drop your things in your room, Mr. Neufeld, and wash up. By then supper will be ready."

"Thank you, Mrs. Grobowitz." Though his hands were full, Mr. Neufeld managed one of his little half bows from the waist. "It smells so good in here. To tell you the truth, the reason I left the other place is that the poor landlady hadn't any idea at all about cooking. Starving to death, I couldn't have eaten what she put in front of me."

Grandma's voice was heavy with sweetness. "I don't think you'll have to worry about anything like that around here, Mr. Neufeld." Then she added with a nod toward the rocking chair, "Now I'd like you to meet my daughter, Berenice."

Mr. Neufeld gave Berenice his awkward little bow

too. "How do you do, Miss Grobowitz," he said.

"Oh, hello," Berenice replied, startled.

"Don't you stand up when you're introduced?" Grandma scolded.

"That's all right, Mrs. Grobowitz," Mr. Neufeld said. Hastily he crossed the kitchen, carrying his bags into his room, where he shut the door behind him.

"Oi, Berenice," Grandma complained, "sometimes you act like a Cossack."

"Oh, Mama, he's just a boarder."

"*Ssh.* . . . He can hear you."

Berenice lowered her voice to a whisper, but Berenice's whisper was the kind you could have heard all the way to Coney Island. "I don't understand why you let the room to a man. You've never done that before."

Grandma shrugged. "In the middle of the year, where am I going to find a schoolteacher? Only a sewing-machine operator could I find, and their work is too seasonal. People like that are always behind with the rent. This man, he's a watchmaker, he works for a big jewelry store on Flatbush Avenue, his rent will be on time." Then, suddenly, her voice dropped to a whisper too—a real whisper. "I'm getting from him two dollars more than I got from Mrs. Ackerman. He must make very good wages."

Berenice couldn't argue with two dollars a week. She rose from the rocker as Lilly walked back into the kitchen. "Wait 'til you meet the new boarder," she said to her sister. "You'll forget all about Morrie Weissbinder." With a lift of her eyebrows, she sailed into the bathroom to wash up for supper.

"What does she mean?" Lilly asked eagerly. "Is he young? Is he handsome?"

I giggled.

"Handsome is as handsome does," Grandma intoned. She was very fond of wise sayings. No matter what the situation, she always managed to come up with one. They didn't always quite fit.

"Then he must have money," Lilly said, sitting down at the table. "Old, ugly, and rich."

"*Ssh* . . ." Grandma scolded her as she had Berenice a few moments before. "He'll hear you."

I don't know whether Mr. Neufeld had heard or not. He came out of his room then and bowed to Lilly too when Grandma introduced them. But unlike Berenice or me, she rose, held out her hand to him, and shook his very prettily, murmuring softly, "A pleasure to have such a distinguished gentleman with us, Mr. Neufeld. It's certainly a pleasant change from the schoolteachers and bookkeepers we usually get."

"I'm just a watchmaker, Miss Grobowitz," he said as he took his place at the table. "I'm not sure that's any improvement."

"She means," Berenice announced as she walked back into the kitchen, "that anything in pants is an improvement."

"Berenice!" Grandma remonstrated. She put a plate of soup down in front of Mr. Neufeld. "Don't mind them," she said. "You know these modern girls. They're all terrible teases."

"Oh, I like it," Mr. Neufeld said. "I'm glad to be among young people again. It was too quiet at the last place."

After that, Mr. Neufeld didn't say much. With enthusiasm, he ate every drop that was put in front of him. Grandma could see that he'd want seconds. She didn't put a carrot or a piece of meat in my bowl of soup, and that way there was enough left so she could offer him more. He took it, too. When it came to dessert, Grandma didn't even ask. She gave him twice as many stewed pears as she gave Berenice or Lilly, and she didn't give me any.

"You should have some pears, Miss Warshefsky," Mr. Neufeld said to me. "They're delicious."

"There aren't any more," I pointed out.

Mr. Neufeld glanced from his plate to those in front of the aunts to the serving bowl. "You gave me too many," he said to Grandma.

"Oh, no," Grandma replied hastily. "Gertie doesn't like stewed pears. Do you, Gertie?"

"Yes, I like pears," I replied. "I like pears just as much as Aunt Berenice or Aunt Lilly likes pears."

"Last time we had pears," Grandma said with great deliberateness, "you did not like them."

I really couldn't remember how I'd felt about stewed pears the last time. I opened my mouth to say something to that effect, but the look on Grandma's face was enough to make me change my mind. I gulped and shrugged. Mr. Neufeld didn't look convinced, but he ate all the pears in his dish anyway. Then he pushed himself away from the table. "Well, Mrs. Grobowitz, Miss Grobowitz, Miss Grobowitz, Miss Warshefsky," he said, nodding to each of us in turn, "thank you for a delicious meal and, even more, for your delightful company."

"You know, Mr. Neufeld," Berenice said, "it sounds silly for you to call us by our last names, I mean, if you're going to live here and all, like a member of the family. I'm Berenice, she's Lilly, and that's Gertie over there."

34

"Well, thank you, Miss Berenice," Mr. Neufeld replied. "I'm honored." He glanced first at Lilly and then at me. "Is that all right with you, Miss Lilly? Miss Gertrude?"

"Certainly," Lilly said with a graceful nod.

I just giggled a little. Miss Gertrude. Somehow that was even fancier than Miss Warshefsky.

Mr. Neufeld excused himself and went into his room. "Gollee Moses!" Berenice exclaimed when his door had clicked shut. "You picked a strange one this time, Mama. *Miss* Berenice! *Miss* Gertrude!"

"I think he's nice," I said.

"Oh, who asked you?" Lilly said.

"He's educated, that's all," I replied. "Cultured. You're not used to people like that."

"And you are?" Lilly scoffed. "The one with a nut for a mother?"

"That nut is your sister," Grandma reminded her. "Don't forget it." She could say Mama was crazy, but she didn't like to hear it from Lilly or Berenice.

"Half sister," Lilly corrected her. But she wasn't done with me. "A nut for a mother and a criminal for a father," she added.

"A criminal?" I cried furiously. "A criminal? What crime did he ever commit?"

"Desertion is a crime in this state," Berenice responded smugly. "At least, so I've been told." She looked Grandma right in the eye, and Grandma didn't deny it.

"I'm not deserted," I insisted. "He writes to me."

Now it was Grandma's turn. "When was the last letter, Gertie?" she asked. Her tone wasn't angry, just flat, as if she were reading the history lesson out loud. "And when did he last send you so much as a buffalo nickel? If what he did to you and your mother isn't desertion, I don't know what to call it. If I were you, I'd forget about your father and your mother both, and start cleaning up the kitchen."

Just then someone rapped on our front door. Lilly ran through the parlor to get it. "Who's she expecting?" Grandma asked.

"Who do you think?" Berenice shot back.

Sure enough, Morrie Weissbinder followed Lilly back into the kitchen. "Hello, Mrs. Grobowitz," he said to Grandma, flashing her his huge smile. "Do you mind if Lilly comes with me to see the Chaplin movie at the Baronet? I'll get her home by ten. I know there's school tomorrow." He saw the frown on Grandma's face so he added quickly, "I'd like to take Berenice too. The three of us can go."

Grandma probably thought Morrie meant he'd be paying for all three of them. I knew better. I knew that Morrie had an agreement with the aunts. When they went anywhere, they went Dutch, because Morrie was saving up for college. Grandma said a child was entitled to keep half of any money she earned on her own. Since Berenice was the only one with a job, she usually paid for both Lilly and herself. But Grandma didn't know that, so she shrugged and said, "All right. The three of you together, I guess there's no harm in that." She didn't add anything about homework. That wasn't one of the things that mattered to her.

So Berenice and Lilly went off with Morrie, and Grandma went upstairs to sit with her friend, Mrs. Augustine. I was piling the dishes in the sink when Mr. Neufeld came out of his bedroom, carrying a large black book in his hand.

"Do you mind if I sit in this rocker and read?" he asked. "The light isn't so good in my room."

"Go right ahead," I said, "if the clatter of the dishes doesn't bother you."

"Oh, it won't bother me," he assured me.

I kept on working as I talked. "I'm sure if you ask Grandma, she'll let you have one of the lamps from the front room to read by."

Mr. Neufeld smiled. "Then I won't have an excuse to come out here for some company, will I?"

I smiled too. "All right. I won't say anything to Grandma if you don't."

"Where is your grandmother?" Mr. Neufeld inquired.

"She went upstairs to visit her friend, Mrs. Augustine. She does that almost every night after supper. They sit and knit."

"And your aunts?" he went on.

"They went to the movies. They went to see Charlie Chaplin, with Morrie Weissbinder."

"And you, Miss Gertrude? Don't you like Charlie Chaplin?"

"I like him," I admitted. "I went to see him once with my father. But I can't go now. I don't have any money. Besides, I have to clean up the kitchen."

"And they don't? Your aunts, I mean."

"No. They don't." The dishes were all washed now and ranged neatly in the rack. I opened a drawer in the cupboard, took out a dish towel, and started to dry.

"Do you have another towel?" Mr. Neufeld asked. "I can help you."

"Thanks," I said, "but no thanks. If Grandma came down and saw you drying, she'd murder me."

"I'll tell her it was my idea," he offered.

I shook my head. "That wouldn't make any difference. Just stay where you are and keep talking. It helps pass the time."

But for a few moments Mr. Neufeld didn't say anything at all. He took a packet of peppermint drops out of his pocket and popped a couple of them in his mouth. Only after he had sucked on them for a while did he speak again. "If your aunts helped you, you'd get done much faster."

Did he think I was some kind of dummy? "I know that, Mr. Neufeld," I responded tartly. "People may think my mother is a lunatic, but I'm certainly not crazy."

Now what in the world had made me say that? Well, he wouldn't live long in our house without finding out all about it anyway, so what difference did it make that I had told him? "I'm sorry," he said gently. "I'm sorry that your mother is ill. And your father? I trust he's well."

"Oh, he's fine, I guess," I responded casually. "He's out West, I think. The last letter was from Denver, Colorado. Kessler's Boarding House, Denver, Colorado. He'll come back for me when he's made his fortune."

"That'll be nice," Mr. Neufeld replied, his voice still quiet. "When was he in Denver?"

"Maybe he's still there," I said. My voice was as quiet as his. "The last letter was in August. But he'll come back for me. I know it. He promised."

Mr. Neufeld nodded without saying anything.

I went on quickly. "But you see, since he doesn't send money, I guess it really was good of Grandma to let me come here to live. She doesn't have so much herself, and we three girls eat a lot, like three Shleppermans, Grandma says."

"Shleppermans?"

"That's Mr. Goldfarb's horse. Mr. Goldfarb is the milkman."

"Oh, I see."

"At least Grandma didn't make me to go to the orphanage." I wanted to be fair. "Sadie Weil and her little brother had to go to the orphanage, after their mother died. No one ever saw them again."

"Maybe Sadie Weil and her little brother are better off than you think," Mr. Neufeld said. "I was in an orphanage in Europe for a while when I was a boy. It wasn't so bad. They had some good teachers there, and one of them taught me to read and write. He even gave me a Yiddish Bible for my very own when I left."

I was interested to find out that Mr. Neufeld hadn't always been a watchmaker who earned a good salary and owned two boxes full of books. But I was still scared of the orphanage. "I wouldn't be going to your orphanage," I pointed out. "I'd just disappear into the one they sent Sadie to, and I'd never be heard of again. Sadie probably isn't even there anymore herself. She's probably dead by now."

"I doubt that," Mr. Neufeld commented. "You surely would have heard."

"I guess so," I agreed reluctantly. "But anyway, everyone knows the orphanage is terrible, and no matter how bad it is here, it's better than there, and Grandma keeps me even though she doesn't like my father. She didn't want Mama to marry him. She said he's a gambler and too handsome. I can't quite understand why she holds his looks against him."

Mr. Neufeld shook his head as if to say he couldn't imagine why either.

I was drying the knives and dropping them, clang, clang, clang, into the meat silverware drawer. "To tell you the truth," I said, "I don't think Grandma liked my mother's papa too much either. She liked her second husband better, Mr. Grobowitz, the one who was Berenice and Lilly's father. She says her first husband and Mama were nothing but trouble, trouble, trouble, right from the start, and now here she is with me on her hands. But that's not my fault."

"No, of course it isn't," Mr. Neufeld agreed. "However, I don't suppose it's anyone else's, either." The brown eyes behind his thick gold-rimmed lenses looked thoughtfully into mine.

I dried my hands and hung up the dish towel. "I'm going to my room to get my books," I told him. "Then I'll come back." I glanced over the floor. I didn't see many crumbs. If I skipped sweeping, maybe Grandma wouldn't notice. "My teacher gave me a book to read," I told Mr. Neufeld. "I want to get through my homework fast so I can start it."

"You like books." It was a statement, not a question.

I nodded. "I like school too," I added suddenly. "Grandma wants me to quit, but I don't want to."

"I don't blame you," Mr. Neufeld agreed.

I ran out of the room then, got my books, and brought them back into the kitchen. Mr. Neufeld was absorbed in his large black volume. I sat down at the kitchen table and began my homework. It didn't take me long. Then I pushed it aside and picked up *Daddy Long Legs*. Mr. Neufeld must have seen me do that out of the corner of his eye. "What's the name of your book," he asked me, "and who wrote it?"

"*Daddy Long Legs* by Jean Webster. What about yours?"

"Come here and look."

I left my chair and went over to the rocker in which he was sitting. The book he was reading was written in a language I couldn't understand, but I recognized the letters. "It's Yiddish," I said.

He shook his head. "No, Hebrew. Can't you read Hebrew?"

"No," I admitted. "Grandma isn't religious. I mean, the house is kosher and all that, but we hardly ever go to the synagogue."

"You should know how to read Hebrew," Mr. Neufeld said, his hand slamming down on the open page of his book. "Every Jew should. I'll teach you."

"My parents aren't religious either," I explained.

"Religion has nothing to do with it," Mr. Neufeld replied. "It's a matter of being properly educated as a Jew. I will teach you."

"It looks very hard."

"Anything worth knowing is hard to learn. Once you get into it, you'll enjoy it, it won't seem so hard."

I shrugged. I wasn't at all sure I wanted to give up reading *Daddy Long Legs* in order to learn to read

Hebrew, and I didn't see how I could do both, but I decided to try it anyhow. Knowing another thing couldn't do any harm.

"We'll start tomorrow evening," Mr. Neufeld said. "I'll pick up a primer on my lunch hour so I can teach you the aleph-bes, the alphabet."

"All right." I went back to the table and started reading *Daddy Long Legs* as fast as I could. I liked it. It was about an orphan who gets sent to college by a rich man. All she has ever seen of him is his shadow, so she calls him Daddy Long Legs and writes him letters in which she pours out all her inner feelings, even though he never answers her. Of course, I wasn't an orphan, but I understood how she felt. Once she got to college, it didn't take her very long to imagine she was just as good as anyone else.

THREE

Every night after I'd cleaned up the kitchen and done my homework, I studied Hebrew with Mr. Neufeld. I managed to learn to read the letters, but not much more. It was just as hard as I had thought it was going to be. But I learned a lot of other things from Mr. Neufeld. Every word in the primer, sometimes even just a letter, sent him off on a long digression, usually some sort of story from the Bible, or Jewish history, or legend. Everything reminded him of something else. He knew more than any other person I had ever met, including Miss Needham.

Of all the stories he told me, I liked the one about Queen Esther the best. I knew about the holiday of Purim, which honors Queen Esther, because although Grandma didn't go to shul very often, she went on some holidays, and the previous year she'd taken the three of us to hear the story of Esther read out loud from the scroll. They had read it in Hebrew, and I hadn't understood a word of it. I had recognized the name of Haman, though, each time the cantor had chanted it, and I'd shaken my noisemaker as loud as anyone when I'd heard it. So I had had fun even though I couldn't follow the plot.

But when Mr. Neufeld told the story of Esther, he told it in such a wonderful way that I almost learned it by heart. I loved it more than any other story I'd ever heard, or read, including *Daddy Long Legs*, which turned out to be very good too. In *Daddy Long Legs*, the orphan falls in love with a relative of one of her college chums, and in the end he proves to be none other than Daddy Long Legs! But the story of Esther was even better.

It was so good that the night he told it to me, Lilly and Berenice listened too. Grandma had gone upstairs. Lilly had put a mudpack on her face and Berenice was working on a skirt she'd brought from Mrs. Wagner's.

Mrs. Wagner was paying her an extra dime to finish it at home. The four of us were in the kitchen, Berenice and Lilly at the table, and me perched on a stool I'd pulled up next to the rocker in which Mr. Neufeld sat.

"What letter is this?" Mr. Neufeld asked, pointing to an odd-looking creature with a dot in the middle of it. "Remember, we talked about it Monday night?"

I stared at it a long minute. "It sounds like a *p*," I said at last. Except for the dot in the middle, it looked just like the letter which made the *f* sound. I had to think to remember which was which.

Mr. Neufeld's face broke into a broad smile. "That's right!" he exclaimed. "Oh, you have a wonderful memory, Gertie. I'm so proud of you. It sounds like a *p*, and it's called a 'pay.' What word begins with a 'pay'?"

"Really, Mr. Neufeld," I said, "how would I know something like that?"

"You see," Lilly interjected, "she's not so smart after all."

Mr. Neufeld pretended he hadn't heard her. "It's a holiday, Gertie, a famous holiday."

"Purim!" Berenice shouted triumphantly.

"Very good, Berenice," Mr. Neufeld congratulated her. "And do you know why we celebrate Purim, Berenice?"

"Something to do with Esther and Haman," Berenice muttered, putting her head down close to her sewing. "I don't remember the details."

"Do you, Gertie?" Mr. Neufeld asked me. "Purim is coming soon—it's only six weeks away. I'll be very glad to see it. Passover and spring are never far behind Purim." He went into the loud, ringing tone he used when he quoted something directly. " 'For lo! the winter is over and done, and the voice of the turtle is heard in the land.' That's from the Song of Songs, in the Bible, Gertie. We say it on Passover during the Seder. Do you remember? Pesach begins with a 'pay' too."

"Go back to Esther," I urged. "We don't remember the details. You tell us."

So Mr. Neufeld told us the details. Even Lilly looked up from the love story she was reading in the New York *Journal* and listened. The story of Esther and King Ahasuerus was a better love story. It was a Cinderella story, and I'd always liked them best. Not that Esther was badly treated by Mordecai, the cousin whom she had lived with ever since her parents had died, the way Cinderella was by her stepmother and stepsisters. Mordecai loved Esther and was good to her, but they were Jewish, so everybody else in Persia looked down on them. But that didn't stop the king from falling in love with her, because she was so good and so beautiful, and from choosing her for his wife out of a thousand other incredibly lovely girls. And then, because she was queen, she was able to save all the Jews from being destroyed by the king's wicked prime minister, Haman, who hated all the Jews because Mordecai wouldn't bow down to him, but only to God. It took a lot of courage for Esther to let the king know how evil Haman was, because in that country in those days not even the queen was allowed to appear before the king unless she'd been invited. Esther knew what had happened to Vashti, the previous queen, when *she'd* disobeyed the king. But Esther went to Ahasuerus anyway, invited him to a banquet, and told him the truth, and then it was Haman who was destroyed instead of the Jews, and Esther who got a book in the Bible with her name on it and became famous forever.

Mr. Neufeld didn't tell the story the way it was written in the Bible. He told it his own way, acting out all the different parts as he went along. The way he told it, it was not only romantic and exciting, it was, at times, even funny. And it took him a long time to tell it, maybe an hour. But we were fascinated from beginning to end. It was as good as the picture show.

When he had finished, I felt like applauding. I smiled at him instead and nodded my head. He smiled back at me, and then he smiled at Berenice and Lilly.

"That's a wonderful story," I said. "Thank you, Mr. Neufeld."

"Yes, thank you," Lilly agreed. "I liked it too."

"It's interesting, isn't it?" Mr. Neufeld said. "It's interesting that the jolliest and gayest of all Jewish holidays is celebrated in honor of a woman, a woman who triumphed over a powerful, wicked man who would have destroyed our people. You won't forget that, will you?"

"Oh, no," I assured him. "I won't forget. Not ever. And she was an orphan too."

"You're not an orphan," Berenice said. "You remind us of that often enough."

"Did I say I was?" I retorted. "I only said that Esther was."

"And *you* might just as well be," Lilly chimed in.

I sat straight up on my stool. "If a person's mother is ill," I announced with all the dignity I could muster, "and a person's father is away on business, that's not a person's fault. It's better than having a father who's dead!"

Well, that shut Lilly and Berenice up, for the moment anyway. Besides, Grandma came in then and shooed all three of us off to bed.

Other nights, Mr. Neufeld told me other stories. He told me about Joseph and his coat of many colors, and how his brothers were jealous of him and sold him into slavery, but he got his revenge years later when he was the most important man in Egypt next to the king, and saved everyone from dying of hunger. He told me about Moses and how he led the Jews out of slavery in Egypt to a new home in the Promised Land. And he told me about David, the greatest of the Jewish kings, who could manage huge armies and a mighty nation, but not his own household. He told me maybe fifty different stories out of the Bible, but none that I loved so well as the story of Esther.

He would have told all the stories to Lilly and Berenice too, but usually they weren't around in the evening to listen, or else they got bored and went off to the bedroom to gossip, read dime novels, and fix each other's hair. The story of Esther was their favorite too.

When they went out, they usually went out with Morrie Weissbinder. He came to the house to get them. It was Lilly he liked, but he took Berenice along too, as a kind of chaperone, to satisfy Grandma. Sometimes his friend Mel Riesman came with him, to take Berenice off his hands and give him time alone with Lilly. I liked Mel. I liked him better than Morrie, even if he wasn't as good looking.

My birthday was February 15, the day after Valentine's Day. The year before, I'd gotten a letter from my father for my birthday, and there'd been a dollar inside of it. I was looking forward to that happening again, because Valentine's Day at school was terrible. I got four valentines, one from Miss Needham, and one from each of the three students who, like Miss Needham, sent a valentine to everyone in the class. I really wasn't too surprised about that, since I myself sent only two valentines—one to Miss Needham and one to Ellen O'Grady. But I felt really bad that Ellen didn't send me a valentine. I had thought Valentine's Day was a good chance for us to make up. Obviously, she didn't agree.

Morrie and Mel came over after supper with a bag of candy hearts for all of us. Morrie had already sent Lilly a great big store-bought valentine card with a lot of lace and gilt on it. It was signed "Guess Who?", but Lilly knew perfectly well whom it had come from. It must have cost a quarter. A card *and* candy. Grandma couldn't accuse him of being cheap that day.

But maybe it was Mel who had bought the candy.

Anyway, it was he who passed it from one of us to the other, urging each of us to help ourselves to a second and third piece after the first.

"Not me," Mr. Neufeld sighed. "It's bad for my teeth. Thank you anyway." But before Mel could take the bag away, Mr. Neufeld's hand shot out and seized a piece. "I am, however, very partial to pink hearts." He bit it, instead of just sucking it, the way you're supposed to. "Pink hearts are bad for my teeth," he said, "but they're good for my soul. Thank you once again, Mr. Riesman, and you too, Mr. Weissbinder." Without getting up from his seat, Mr. Neufeld gave a kind of half bow in the direction of the boys. Berenice giggled.

Mel had placed the bag on the table. I was still drying the dishes, but I reached over and grabbed another heart before Lilly and Berenice ate them all.

"I like Valentine's Day," Lilly announced. "It breaks up the winter a little bit. Winter is so long and boring. I wish it were spring already."

"If St. Valentine's Day comes, can Purim be far behind?" Mr. Neufeld asked. Then he laughed. Putting a Christian holiday like St. Valentine's Day and a Jewish holiday like Purim together in one sentence struck him as funny, but no one else saw the joke.

"The Brownsville Talmud Torah is putting on a Purim play this year," Morrie said. "My mother's in charge."

"That's nice," Grandma said. "We can go see it if they don't charge too much. I sent the girls there for a few months when their father was alive. They ought to let me in for nothing."

"My mother says I have to try out for it," Morrie told us. "I don't want to, but she says I have to. She says the only way she got Miss Katz to direct the show was by promising her there'd be boys to play Mordecai and Haman and Ahasuerus and all the other parts. She's making Mel try out too."

"Miss Katz?" Grandma asked. "So who's Miss Katz?"

"She lives over on Eastern Parkway," Mel explained. "She teaches English at Thomas Jefferson High School." That was the high school Berenice, Lilly, Morrie, and Mel all went to.

"Does she teach at the Talmud Torah too?" I asked.

"Of course not, dummy," Berenice said. "She doesn't even know Hebrew. You don't have to be a teacher or a student at the Brownsville Talmud Torah to work on the play. It's just for their benefit. It's a way for them to raise money. Isn't that right, Morrie?"

Morrie nodded.

"And a very good way too," Mr. Neufeld approved. "Purim has been celebrated with Purimspeils, with theatrical performances, since the Middle Ages."

Lilly poked Berenice, and Berenice giggled again. They didn't have any respect for Mr. Neufeld's superior knowledge.

"I don't know about that," Morrie said, "but if my mother's behind it, you can be sure it'll be done right—scenery and costumes and all that stuff."

"What part do you think you'll play, Morrie?" Lilly asked.

Morrie shrugged. "That's up to Miss Katz, but I suppose I'll be Mordecai or Ahasuerus." Undue modesty wasn't one of Morrie's problems.

"And who will be Esther?" Lilly asked.

Morrie shrugged again. "How do I know? Lots of girls'll try out, that much I do know."

"Including Mildred Levy?" Lilly asked. Mildred Levy lived in the same building as Morrie. They'd played together when they were little, and Lilly had an idea that Mildred would have liked the games to continue.

"Yeah, sure," Morrie replied casually.

"She's not pretty enough for Esther," Lilly said.

"Well, if she isn't," Morrie offered with a lift of his eyebrows and a broad grin, "I'd like to know who is."

He was teasing Lilly, of course. After the valentine card, she should have realized that. But Lilly wasn't very good at taking a joke. She flushed a bright red and pressed her lips together. We all knew what she was thinking. "Lilly would like to try out for Esther, wouldn't you, Lilly?" Berenice said.

Lilly sniffed.

"Well, I know I would," Berenice said. "Can I?"

"Sure. Why not?" Morrie said.

"Well, if you can, then I certainly can," Lilly said. "You're too tall to be Queen Esther. You can be Queen Vashti."

"*You* can be Queen Vashti," Berenice retorted. "I'll be Queen Esther."

"It's not up to you to decide," I pointed out. "It's up to Miss Katz."

"Don't you get any big ideas, dummy," Berenice said. "You can't try out. I bet you have to be in high school to be in it. This isn't some tacky little production thrown together at some cheder with a bunch of little kids. It's high class."

I slammed down the pot I was drying and marched

over to the table. "How do you know?" I waved my dish towel in her face.

"I'm afraid she's right," Mel said, his voice gentle. "Miss Katz said she didn't want to get involved with little kids. If she did, she'd just use the Talmud Torah students. But she's not used to them. She says they're too noisy. So it has to be high-school kids. She's directed a lot of plays at Thomas Jefferson. Mrs. Weissbinder was very happy to get her."

"I'm not a little kid," I insisted. "I'm nearly as tall as Lilly, and not much younger."

"Two years," Lilly interposed quickly.

"A year and a half," I retorted.

"We all know you're not little," Mel appeased me. "But that's Miss Katz's rule. You have to be in ninth grade at least to be in the show."

"She couldn't be in it anyway," Grandma said. "She has too much to do as it is."

I knew it was silly to even imagine trying out for the part of Queen Esther, let alone getting it, but I couldn't help feeling disappointed anyway. Later, when the boys had left, Grandma had gone upstairs, the aunts were in their room, and I was left alone with Mr. Neufeld, I said as much. "Well, look at it this way," he tried to comfort me. "You didn't have enough time to get really excited about the play, so you can't really be let down. Think about poor Lilly. She's got her heart set on playing the part of Esther, and how much chance does she actually have of getting it, with all the girls in Brownsville trying out? Just imagine how disappointed *she's* going to be."

I nodded my head. "Very," I agreed. "She's used to having her own way. But she doesn't know anything about acting."

"I'm sure she doesn't," Mr. Neufeld responded. "But then, who does? Do you?"

"Oh, not really," I admitted. "But sometimes, in my head, I have the feeling that my whole life is a play or a story, and I'm acting it out."

"You're the heroine," Mr. Neufeld said, "and your grandmother and your aunts are the villains."

He had said it, not me. I didn't answer.

"Who's the prince?" Mr. Neufeld asked. "Who's the fairy godmother?"

I shook my head.

"Maybe they don't exist in real life," Mr. Neufeld said. "Maybe villains don't either."

"Haman was a real villain," I reminded him. "And Esther was a real heroine. Unless you don't think the stories in the Bible are true."

"They're true enough," Mr. Neufeld said.

Later on, when I was in bed, I realized I wasn't exactly sure what he'd meant by that remark. After I fell asleep I dreamed I really was Queen Esther, wearing a diamond crown and eating bags and bags of pink valentine hearts.

FOUR

Anyway, what happened the next day, my birthday, made the disappointment I'd felt about not being allowed to try out for the Brownsville Talmud Torah's Purimspeil seem extremely unimportant.

No one said "Happy Birthday" to me at breakfast. Mr. Neufeld didn't know it was my birthday, the aunts had forgotten, if they had ever known, and Grandma didn't mention it because she didn't think birthdays were important. Mama and Papa hadn't felt that way. When I had lived with them, I'd always had a birthday cake and a party with a lot of kids. But that was in the old neighborhood, and I didn't know what those kids were doing now, except for Sadie Weil, who, I guessed, was still in the orphanage, if she wasn't dead.

After breakfast, Berenice and Lilly went to school, but not me. I was taking the day off. Grandma was bringing me to Queens to visit my mother in the hospital. She did that every three or four months.

It was a long ride on the subway and elevated trains from Brooklyn to Queens. We had to change twice. Grandma knit to pass the time. I studied my Hebrew primer and when I got bored with that, I stared at the other people in the car. After a while, I tugged at Grandma's sleeve.

She turned her head toward me. "What is it, Gertie?"

"Do you think Mama's better? Do you think she'll know us this time?"

Grandma shook her head. "People don't usually get better there," she said. "They stay the same, or they get worse. If she was better, I think the hospital would tell me."

"Oh." I fixed my eyes on the man sitting opposite me. He had a long, tangled black beard and I tried to imagine what it would have been like to be no bigger than a grain of salt and live in that beard, along with a whole lot of other tiny people.

But Grandma was talking again, and I had to listen. "I decided on today to visit your mother for a reason, though," Grandma said. "Maybe she has some kind of memory of the day you were born. Maybe seeing you today will bring it back to her."

"I thought you didn't think birthdays were important."

"The day a person is born is important for the person and for the person's mother." Grandma's voice was dry and flat. "But is that any excuse for spending a lot of money on presents or for eating too much? Even when their father was alive, I didn't fuss over Lilly or Berenice's birthdays." Abruptly she turned back to her knitting. "Now we certainly can't afford that kind of silly business." She didn't say much more for the rest of the trip, and I didn't either.

When we got off the train we still had to walk about a mile to Broadmere State Hospital. It was a huge place, spread over acres and acres of ground. But by this time Grandma and I knew where to go. We entered the building in which Mama lived. Grandma spoke to the guard at the desk in the lobby, and then we went upstairs to the day room on the third floor. It was full of women, all wearing identical blue cotton dresses fastened with ties. Some of the women were knitting or crocheting. A few were seated at tables, playing cards. A couple of them were talking to each other, but most just sat, staring vacantly at a wall or into the middle of the room. Two attendants stood in a corner, watching. This was a ward for the harmless, quiet inmates of the hospital, so they didn't waste money on a lot of help for them.

I glanced rapidly from one figure to another, but Mama wasn't in the room. Grandma noticed that too and went over to one of the attendants. "We've come to visit Mrs. Warshefsky," she said. "Please, could you bring her here?" We weren't allowed to visit patients in their rooms, only in the day room. And we weren't allowed to come any time we wanted. Tuesdays and Sundays were the only times visitors were permitted. And on that Tuesday morning we were the only visitors in the room.

"All right, I'll get her," the attendant said. "But you'd better wait for her out in the hall. Some of the loonies'll bother you if you stay in here. Babble to you, you know, or pull at your clothes."

"That's all right," I said. "We'll wait right here." And I sat down in the nearest chair. Grandma shot me a curious look, but she decided not to object. She sat down too.

The attendant shrugged. "Suit yourselves," she said, and left.

Grandma and I were sitting at a table. Two other women were there. One of them looked to be about my mother's age, in her early thirties perhaps. Her hair was neatly combed and she wore tiny gold earrings. She looked up at us and smiled. She was pretty when she smiled. "Good morning," she said.

"Good morning," I replied.

"Is it nice out?" she asked.

"Not really," I replied. "The sun is shining, but it's very windy."

"I used to go for walks in the wind," she said. "I didn't mind. The wind makes you feel clean, and full of energy."

"I guess it's all right if you have a really warm coat."

"Your coat is warm." Grandma's voice was sharp.

"I didn't say it wasn't," I replied. It was warm enough, I guess. Berenice had handed it down to Lilly and Lilly had handed it down to me.

"Who are you visiting?" the woman asked.

"Miriam Warshefsky," I said. "She's my mother. Do you know her?"

The woman nodded, but she didn't say anything.

"You talk too much, Gertie," Grandma said. She turned to the woman. "Don't mind her," she added.

"It's nice to talk to someone different," the woman said. "My friend here doesn't have much to say." It was true that the other woman, somewhat older, hadn't yet uttered a single word. "We play cards, though, sometimes," the first woman continued, as if she didn't want us to think her disloyal to her friend. "She's very good at cards." One of the women was talkative and the other one was silent, but neither of them seemed crazy to me.

Then the attendant came into the room, holding Mama by the hand. It took me a moment to recognize her, she had gotten so thin. But maybe she had been thin the last time I'd visited her too, only I hadn't remembered. In my mind, I always saw her as she had been before she got sick.

The attendant led Mama to our table and, with her hand on Mama's shoulder, pushed Mama down into a chair. "We'll leave you alone," the talkative lady said, "so you can visit." She got up from her seat. "Come along, Mrs. Wilson," she said to the silent woman. "We'll go look outside for a while. Maybe we'll see a robin." Mrs. Wilson got up obediently and followed her to the window, where they stood peering through the glass as if there were something else beyond it besides grim brick hospital buildings and treeless lawns covered with brownish yellow winter grass.

I looked at Mama. Her light brown hair was stringy and uncombed. Her blue cotton dress was wrinkled. I recognized the felt slippers she had on her feet. They had been new when we had lived together, but now they had holes in them. "Grandma," I said, "we ought to buy Mama a new pair of slippers."

Grandma didn't answer me. She leaned over and put her face close to Mama's. She spoke in a loud, clear voice. "Hello, Miriam," she said. "How are you today?"

Mama turned her head away from Grandma and looked right at me.

"Hello, Mama," I said. "Do you know me? I'm Gertie. Today's my birthday."

Mama smiled. Two of her teeth were missing. I was sure she had had all her teeth the last time I'd seen her. She reached out and touched my hair, which was light brown and soft, like hers. "Pretty," she said. "You're a pretty girl. I had a child once, but she died."

"No, she didn't," I cried out. "She didn't die. That child is me, and I'm alive. I'm your child. I'm Gertie. Don't you know me?"

Mama was still smiling. "My baby died," she said. She didn't sound upset, or angry. Her voice was soft and calm. "My baby died."

I couldn't help it. I grabbed her wrist with my hand and shook her arm. "I'm Gertie, I'm Gertie," I insisted. "You must know who I am. You must."

With surprising strength, Mama pulled her arm out of my grip. Mrs. Wilson and the talkative lady had turned away from the window and were staring at us. Some of the other people in the room were staring too, though many hadn't moved a muscle since we'd come in. "I want some candy," Mama said. "Do you have some candy?"

Grandma opened her knitting basket and pulled out a bag of penny candy. Mama grabbed the bag and seized a handful. In a flash, her mouth was so full she couldn't talk at all.

The attendant came over to our table. "Now, Miriam," she said, "I'll have to keep this candy for you. Otherwise, you'll eat it all at once and get sick." She turned to Grandma. "I thought I told you last time not to bring candy."

"No one ever told me anything," Grandma said. "You weren't even here last time I came. Other nurses were here."

"Well, it's a rule," the attendant said. "No candy." Mama was clutching the bag, but the attendant pulled at her fingers until she released it, and then she put the bag in the pocket of her uniform. Mama started to cry. "Now, now, Miriam," the attendant said, "you can have some later. I'll give you some later."

Mama stood up. With one hand she grabbed the attendant's arm and with the other she reached into the pocket where the candy had disappeared. But though Mama was strong, the attendant was stronger. With her free hand she pushed Mama away. The other attendant crossed the room quickly and seized Mama from behind. Her face was so full of fury you'd think Mama had murdered someone.

"She's getting wild," the first attendant said. "We'll have to take her back to her room." She turned to Grandma. "Sometimes," she said angrily, "I think visitors' days should be canceled entirely. They only upset our routine." She handed the candy to the second attendant, and then, holding Mama's arm very tightly, marched her out of the room.

"Goodbye, Mama," I called as they walked out the door. But Mama didn't hear, or if she heard, didn't pay any attention. She was still weeping over her lost candy.

Grandma turned to the second attendant. "That's Mrs. Warshefsky's candy," she said. "She'd better get it."

"If she's good," the second attendant said, "she'll get a piece each night after supper. And if she's not good, she won't get any at all. Those are the rules."

"Let's go, Gertie," Grandma said. She took my hand and we too started toward the door. But before we could get through it, I felt a tap on my shoulder. I turned. It was the woman who had spoken to us when we had first come in, the woman who liked the wind. "I'm sorry, dear," she whispered. "I'm sorry. Next time she'll be better, I'm sure."

But I knew she wouldn't be. Nothing was going to happen that would make her better. I felt tears welling up in my eyes. I knew in a minute they'd start to fall, so I just shook my head without saying anything and ran out of the room.

I'll say one thing for Grandma. Much as she liked wise sayings, she knew when to keep her mouth shut. She didn't say a word as we walked down the stairs, out of the building, across the wide, empty, frozen yard, and through the big iron gates. We were both silent until we got on the train and were rattling along on our way home to Brooklyn. I was crying. I had started crying as soon as we had left the day room, and I hadn't yet stopped. My handkerchief was soaked through.

Grandma took a clean one out of her basket and handed it to me. "Nu, Gertie, get hold of yourself," she ordered. "There's nothing you can do about it. Nothing at all."

"Oh, Grandma," I wailed, "why is she like that? How did she get like that?"

Grandma shook her head. "She was always weak and silly," she replied. "She married your father because he was handsome and charming. I knew he was no good the day he walked through the door." Her tone was full of bitterness. "I warned her. She wouldn't listen. And when she found out for herself what he really was, she couldn't take it. She fell apart. She went back to being a baby, and left her own baby on my hands."

I was angry enough now to stop crying. "My father isn't no good," I said. "He never did anything bad."

"Nothing he could be put in jail for," Grandma said, "like he should have been."

"Grandma, what do you mean?" She was always throwing out dark hints about my father. I thought it was about time she told me what she meant.

"When you're older, Gertie, you'll know," Grandma said. "He wasn't nice to your mother. He wasn't the kind of husband he should have been."

I didn't press her any further. Maybe I really didn't want to know the bad things he'd done. He'd always been wonderful to me, full of games, and treats, and stories. And if he had argued with my mother, I'd never heard it.

But Grandma went on about him anyway. He was one of her favorite subjects. "You know he's irresponsible. You know he doesn't send any money for you."

She never let me forget. It didn't require comment.

"So you can see for yourself," she droned on, "if not for me, you'd be in the orphanage."

I blew my nose and dabbed at my eyes.

"You understand, Gertie," Grandma added, in her first attempt in all the time I'd known her to explain herself, "I don't want you to go to the orphanage. I want you to stay with me. But where's the money to support you supposed to come from? You'll just have to quit school soon and go to work. You've already had a lot more schooling than I ever had, and I get along."

I crumpled up my handkerchief. "Maybe there'll be a letter from my father when we get home," I said. "Maybe there'll be some money in it."

"Stop dreaming, Gertie," Grandma said.

I knew she was right. How could I hope for anything after such a morning as we'd just had? It was my birthday, and instead of being better than other days, it was worse. There was no letter from my father in the mailbox. The only thing in the mailbox was a bill from the gas company. I handed it to Grandma, and then I ran upstairs into the bedroom. I threw myself on my cot and cried some more. After a while Grandma came in and told me to come to the kitchen for some lunch.

"I'm not hungry," I said.

"Yes, you are," she told me. "I know. Eat some lunch, you'll feel better. And then get started. You got work to do."

So I ate lunch and then I polished all the furniture in the front room while Grandma sat in the kitchen, sewing on her machine. For once, I was glad about the work. I couldn't think too much while I was tugging at heavy pieces of furniture, trying not to break any doodads or knickknacks. Because we hadn't gotten home from Broadmere until after one, I barely got the furniture back into place when it was time to start helping Grandma with dinner. She made chicken, even though it wasn't Friday night.

Later she stood at the stove, dishing the food onto

plates. "It's your birthday, Gertie," she said, "so you can pick the part of the chicken you want."

"I pick the leg," I said.

"But Mama," Lilly protested, "you know that Berenice and I both like dark meat. If you give a leg to Gertie, one of us won't be able to have one."

"I'll solve that problem," Mr. Neufeld said. "I'll eat the other leg. Then Lilly and Berenice won't have to fight over it."

"But Mr. Neufeld," Berenice reminded him, "you always eat white meat."

"Today," Mr. Neufeld said, "today has come over me the feeling that I want dark meat. Like a cloud it's come over me."

"But Mama. . ." Lilly began again.

Grandma picked up my plate and put a leg on it. Then she picked up Mr. Neufeld's plate and put the other leg on it. Lilly threw me a black look from beneath her heavy eyelids, but I pretended not to notice. I ate up every bit of my chicken leg. It was delicious.

After dinner, when the others had gone and I was cleaning up, Mr. Neufeld said, "Why didn't you mention that your birthday was coming up?"

I had thought about telling him. After all, we were good friends now. He had told me all about the little village where he'd been born, and the epidemic that had killed his parents, and his life in the orphanage. And I had told him all about the house on Sackman Street that I'd lived in before my mother got sick and my father went away. But in the end, I hadn't said a thing about my birthday. "I didn't want to sound as if I were asking for a present," I explained.

"Well, then, why didn't someone else tell me?" he asked.

"Grandma doesn't believe in birthdays."

"But she gave you the chicken leg because it was your birthday."

"Yes," I agreed, "but I don't know why. That was a surprise."

"Well, Gertie," Mr. Neufeld smiled, "besides eating a chicken leg, how did you celebrate?"

I looked up from the dish I was wiping. "I went to see my mother at Broadmere State Hospital," I replied, keeping my voice as flat as I could. I didn't want to start crying in front of him.

"How is she?"

"I don't want to talk about it." I scrubbed hard at the plate with the dish towel.

"All right." He stood up and reached into his pocket. "Well, well," he said, holding up a Hershey bar. "Look what we have here. Bad for my teeth. I hope you'll take it off my hands, Gertie, so I won't be tempted."

"Thanks," I said. It was nice of him to give it to me. I knew how much he liked candy. He was never without licorice sticks or peppermint drops in his pocket. This was the first time, though, that I'd ever seen him pull out a piece of chocolate.

He laid the bar on the table. "It's not much of a birthday present," he said.

"It's better than nothing."

"Well, let's see what else we can come up with." From his other pocket he extracted some change. He spread it out on his palm and stared at it for a moment. Then he picked out the largest coin and handed it to me. It was a quarter. Even my father, when I had lived with him, had never given me a quarter. Maybe pennies now and then, or at most a nickel.

"Gee, Mr. Neufeld, thanks. Thanks a whole lot." I turned the coin over in my hand a few times and then dropped it in my pocket.

"A chicken leg, a chocolate bar, and a quarter. Perhaps, Gertie, things will pick up. I think they'll have to."

I sighed. "They could get worse. I could have to quit school. I could end up in the orphanage." I unwrapped the chocolate bar, broke it, and handed a piece of it to him.

"It's yours," he protested.

"We'll share it," I said. He took it. I knew he couldn't resist. He popped his piece into his mouth, and I slowly chewed on mine. When I was done, I said good night to him and went to bed. I was very, very tired. I didn't even want to stay up to read. All I wanted to do was sleep. And I wanted to be deep, deep asleep before Aunt Berenice and Aunt Lilly came home.

FIVE.

Sunday afternoon I went down to the Brownsville Talmud Torah's assembly room with Grandma, Lilly, and Berenice. I had worked like a fiend all day Saturday, and Sunday morning too. The flat shone, and there wasn't so much as a stocking unwashed. I'd made sure neither Grandma nor the aunts could think of a reason why I couldn't go along, to watch.

At least fifty kids had gathered in that hall. Every one of them had brought a mother or a father, or a brother or a sister, or just a friend, for company. They were all scrambling for seats or calling across the room to someone they knew whom they'd just that minute noticed. Even if they were talking to the person sitting next to them, they had to shout to be heard. Miss Katz and Mrs. Weissbinder were shouting too, trying to create some order in the midst of utter confusion.

Fortunately, though Miss Katz was a small woman, she had a voice stronger than everyone else's put together. She stood on the platform at the end of the room, clapped her hands, and shouted, "Quiet, please. Right now! Quiet." She didn't look anything like Miss Needham. She was dressed in bright silk and her hair was cropped short and held in place with a silk band that matched her dress, like Irene Castle, the dancer. But she had that same kind of authority that Miss Needham possessed. When she wanted your attention, she got it.

At last everyone was quiet. Miss Katz spoke again, this time in a perfectly normal tone of voice. "Each person who wants to be in the play will come up to the platform and recite a piece. I don't care what piece you choose—just make sure it's not more than twenty lines." Her eyes roved about the room. I thought they stopped and looked directly into mine. "I see some children here who are not of high-school age. I'm very sorry, but you can't try out. We don't have much time to get this show together, and I can only use people who can learn their lines quickly and who are old enough to come to rehearsals on school nights." Well, I could certainly learn lines as quickly as Lilly or Berenice, and I stayed up until midnight lots of nights when I had more work than usual and a good book to read besides. But Miss Katz didn't know that, and anyway, she couldn't make exceptions.

"Everyone who tries out will get a part," Miss Katz added. "We need plenty of courtiers, citizens of Shushan, soldiers, Jews and people like that. There will be a place for all of you. There will be some songs in the production too, so you'll all get a chance to sing." She turned to Mrs. Weissbinder, who was sitting at a little table in front of the platform. "As you come up to recite, give your name and address to Mrs. Weissbinder, and tell her what part you think you'd like to play. Who wants to begin?"

All those kids who'd been yelling and shouting at the top of their lungs just a few moments before were now very, very quiet. Again Miss Katz's eyes roamed the room. "If you're afraid to come up here and recite a piece, how can you possibly take a role in a play?" she asked reasonably. A few hands shot up then, and one of them was Berenice's. "All right," Miss Katz said, "you there." She pointed to Berenice. "And then you, and you."

Berenice marched up the aisle to Mrs. Weissbinder's table. Miss Katz trotted down the platform steps and sat herself next to Mrs. Weissbinder. After telling Mrs. Weissbinder her name, Berenice walked up onto the platform. She stood in the middle and recited "The Village Blacksmith" by Henry Wadsworth Longfellow.

> Under a spreading chestnut tree
> The village smithy stands;
> The smith, a mighty man is he,
> With large and sinewy hands. . . .

She recited it perfectly, without stumbling over one single word, even though she'd learned it three years before, in seventh grade, and probably hadn't thought of it since. Her voice was loud and clear. Grandma, Lilly, and I could hear her without any difficulty, even though we were sitting way in the back. But she said the whole thing without any emotion at all, as if she were reading from a shopping list, and she stood with her hands behind her back and her chest thrust forward, stiff as a wooden cigar-store Indian.

There was a scattering of polite applause after she was done, except for Grandma and me, who clapped hard. Lilly didn't clap at all.

"Thank you, Berenice," Miss Katz said. "You may sit down now."

Berenice didn't say a word. She didn't nod or smile. As stiffly as she had stood on the platform, she walked back to her seat.

"That was nice, Berenice," Grandma said. "I was proud of you."

"Yes," I agreed. "You sounded really good, Aunt Berenice."

"Thanks," she said as she sat down, turning her head toward Lilly as if expecting her to say something too. But Lilly maintained a stony silence. She was really angry at Berenice for trying out at all.

One by one the other kids went up to try out. Morrie Weissbinder recited Antony's funeral speech from *Julius Caesar*. He was the best. Mel Riesman wasn't as dramatic, but I could see his eyes sparkling, and I liked the way he looked up there on the platform.

Lilly waited until almost everyone else had tried out before she took her turn. She sashayed down the aisle, nodding and smiling to everyone she knew along the way, as if she already were a big star. When she got up on the platform, she recited a very short poem by Robert Browning, which she had also memorized in the seventh grade. She and Berenice had had Miss Needham too, and one of the few things Miss Needham ever acted enthusiastic about was poetry. But unlike Berenice, Lilly had asked me to get a copy of the poem from Miss Needham, and she'd been practicing it for days.

Lilly recited in a clear, melodious voice. As she spoke the words, she smiled and looked first to one side of the room and then the other.

> The year's at the spring
> And day's at the morn;
> Morning's at seven;
> The hillside's dew-pearled;
> The lark has his wing;
> The snail's in a thorn:
> God's in his heaven—
> All's right in the world.

It was a very short poem, and even so, she had made several mistakes. I knew how it was supposed to go, because I'd held the book while she practiced. Still, no one noticed that she'd said a few words wrong, or if they did, they didn't care, because she looked so pretty and natural up there in front of us, and sounded so lovely. There was nearly as much applause for her when she was done as there had been for Morrie Weissbinder. People didn't know the real Lilly, as I did. But even I had to admit that she was the best-looking girl in the room. She didn't have to worry about Mildred Levy, not for a minute.

When everyone had taken a turn, Miss Katz and Mrs. Weissbinder put their heads together and mumbled to each other for what seemed like an hour. But at last Miss Katz climbed up on the platform again and once more quieted us all down. "Boys and girls," she said, "you were all very good. It was indeed difficult for Mrs. Weissbinder and me to make our choices. Please don't be disappointed if you didn't get the part you wanted. I'm sure you'll all have fun being in the play anyway." She held a piece of paper up in front of her and began to read from it. "Morrie Weissbinder will play Mordecai." It was lucky that Morrie was so obviously the best one, or else some of the parents might have accused his mother of using undue influence. But as it was, the choice was obvious. Everyone applauded.

Miss Katz continued. "Selig Gross will play Haman." Suddenly, as if a puppet master had pulled our strings, we all booed and stamped our feet, just as we did in the synagogue whenever Haman's name was mentioned during Purim services. Miss Katz had to hold up her hands and stamp her own foot to get everyone quiet again. "All right," she said. "That will be enough. Anyone who doesn't behave properly will be thrown out of the play. No second chances. We don't have the time to fool around." She sighed, as if she was already sorry she'd said she'd be in charge.

"All right," she went on. "Mel Riesman will be King Ahasuerus. Lyman Greenspan is the scribe." Then she announced the names of the two conspirators, and of each of Haman's twelve sons. The aunts had pasted bored looks on their faces, as if they didn't care how long it took Miss Katz to get to Esther. But I could see Berenice's fingers tapping on the seat of her chair, and Lilly playing with a lock of her hair the way she always did when she got nervous.

Finally Miss Katz got to the point. For the first time all day she smiled. "Flo Greenfield will be Haman's wife," she said. "Queen Vashti will be played by Mildred Levy, and our Queen Esther, our own Queen Esther, will be Lilly Grobowitz."

Berenice's face drained white, white as snow. Lilly smiled, a satisfied little smile, like the look on a fat cat's face when he's licking cream off his whiskers.

Miss Katz was still talking. "Everyone else will be members of the court or citizens of the town. Some of you will have speaking parts. I'll assign them as we rehearse. The first rehearsal will be Tuesday evening, promptly at seven o'clock, right here in the assembly room. The first thing you'll each have to do is copy out your part, so be sure to bring paper and pencils with you. Thank you. Good night. See you Tuesday."

Berenice stood up and rushed out of the hall before Miss Katz had even finished her little speech. Lilly pretended not to notice. She stood in the back, receiving the congratulations of all who passed her on their way out. Grandma stood next to her, smiling too, as if part of the glory were hers. I stood off to one side and watched both of them. I wondered what it was going to be like in our house the next few weeks. I wondered if Berenice and Lilly would ever speak to each other again.

SIX

After that, Lilly walked around our flat as if she were already dressed in a flowing white robe with a long train and a diamond crown on her head. Berenice refused to be in the play at all. "I'm not going to be any old citizen of Shushan," she said. "If I can't have a speaking part, I don't need to waste my time."

"You're cutting off your nose to spite your face," Grandma said. But Berenice did not relent. Morrie Weissbinder always stopped by to pick up Lilly for rehearsals. Sometimes Mel Riesman and Mildred Levy were with him. Berenice just stood there, her face expressionless as a piece of wood, and watched them go.

But Lilly was so accustomed to being everybody's darling, including Berenice's, that it took a couple of days for her to realize just how angry Berenice was. She actually asked Berenice to help her make Queen Esther's costume from the piece of white silk Miss Katz had given her. Berenice snarled at her, "Make your own costume. I'm not your lady-in-waiting." Then Lilly understood. After that they spoke to each other no more than was absolutely necessary. During the next few weeks, "Pass the potatoes" was about as far as conversation between them went.

Except once. Very early on a Wednesday, the morning after one of the rehearsals, I woke up with a sudden start. A loud thud sending vibrations through the whole room had shocked me into wakefulness. Shivering with fright, I shot up into a sitting position and looked all around the room. Then I stopped being frightened and started laughing. Lilly was lying on the floor. She looked so funny with her nightgown scrunched up around her knees and her face screwed up like a monkey's. At first I couldn't tell if she was going to cry or scream. She settled for screaming. She sat up, pulled down her nightgown, grabbed hold of the bedpost, and hoisted herself up onto her two feet.

Then she leaned over the bed and shook Berenice by the shoulder. "Open your eyes, you lousy thing," she shouted. "Open your eyes. I know you're not asleep. You're just pretending."

Slowly, slowly, Berenice let her eyelids rise a little bit. But I think Lilly was right. I think Berenice was awake all along. If I couldn't sleep through the noise of Lilly's falling out of bed, how could she?

"What's the big idea?" Berenice asked groggily. "Why did you wake me up? It isn't time for school yet."

"I wake *you* up?" Lilly screamed. "I wake you up? You pushed me out of bed. You did it on purpose."

Berenice sat up now, no longer pretending to be anything other than fully awake. "Don't be stupid, Lilly," she said. "You fell out of bed. It wasn't my fault."

"You pushed me."

"Well, if I did, I didn't mean to. You push me in your sleep all the time. You're always taking up more than your half."

"I've never pushed you all the way out of bed," Lilly countered. "You have to do something like that on purpose. There's no other way. You better say you're sorry."

"Well, I'm not sorry," Berenice replied calmly. "I haven't got anything to be sorry for."

Lilly knelt on the bed next to Berenice, grabbed both her shoulders, and began to shake her. "Say you're sorry, say you're sorry," she screamed. She shook Berenice so hard I thought her head would fall off.

Now I was really frightened. "Aunt Lilly, stop it," I cried. "Stop it, stop it."

But she didn't even hear me. She just kept on shaking Berenice and screaming until, suddenly, the door to our room opened and Grandma walked in, her old flannel wrapper pulled around her nightgown and her gray hair in a long braid down her back. Lilly's hair was in a braid down her back too, and Grandma walked right over to her and tugged at the braid so hard that Lilly's hands dropped from Berenice's shoulders and her whole body jerked backward.

"What's the big idea?" Grandma asked. "What's going on here?"

By now Berenice was sobbing so hard she couldn't speak. "What's going on here?" Grandma repeated, pulling again at Lilly's braid. "Mr. Neufeld must think he's living in Broadmere State Hospital."

"She pushed me out of bed," Lilly said.

Berenice swallowed her sobs and managed to mumble a few words. "I did not. She fell, that's all."

"You pushed me," Lilly said, her voice lower than before but still full of venom.

Berenice blew her nose on the bedsheet. Now I'd have to wash it, and it wasn't even Monday. "Don't you get in bed with me ever again, Miss Lilly Grobowitz," Berenice said, "because if you do, I *will* push you out."

"That's fine with me," Lilly retorted, "because I wouldn't sleep in the same bed as you if it was the last bed on earth." She shook herself loose from Grandma's now-relaxed grasp and marched across the room to my cot. "Get up, Gertie," she ordered. "You can sleep with Berenice from now on, and I'll sleep on the cot."

I jumped up quickly before she changed her mind. The cot was just a narrow piece of canvas without a spring or mattress. I slept all right in it because I was always so tired at night that I would have fallen asleep on the floor, but I was happy to have a turn in a real bed.

However, there was no more sleeping that morning, even though there was an hour to go before my usual getting-up time. I lay down next to Berenice and stretched my limbs in the luxury of a soft mattress. I bounced my rear end a little to feel the movement of the springs. Lilly lay down on the cot. Grandma scolded us all once more for good measure and went back to bed. Berenice remained in an upright position, with her shoulders against her pillow, and talked to me. But she was really talking to Lilly. "Some people," she said, "think that because they get an important part in a play, they really are queens. Well, everyone else can treat them like queens if they want, but they can't expect their own sisters to. Or their own nieces. Isn't that right, Gertie?"

I shut my eyes and pretended I had fallen back to sleep. This quarrel was between Aunt Lilly and Aunt Berenice. I didn't have the slightest intention of getting in the middle of it. But for as long as that play was in rehearsal I slept in the double bed with Berenice, and Lilly slept on the cot. And in the evenings, when there was no rehearsal, when Lilly sat in the kitchen trying to memorize her lines, Berenice shut herself in the bedroom.

Since Berenice wouldn't do it, it was I who had to feed Lilly her cues. Even though it cut down on my reading time and on my conversations wtih Mr. Neufeld, I didn't mind. Grandma was usually upstairs with Mrs. Augustine, but Mr. Neufeld listened to us. Miss

Katz had given Lilly a copy of the whole play because her part was so long. Lilly tried to recite Esther's lines and I read all the other roles. I put on a different voice for each one.

"What do you want, Queen Esther?" I'd say in deep, royal Ahasuerus tones. "For whatever you ask, even if it is half my kingdom, I will give it to you."

Then it was Lilly's turn. "If it please the king to grant my request, let the king and Haman come to a banquet that I shall prepare for them, if I have found favor in the king's sight."

For Haman I put on a phony humble voice, with a snarl underneath it. "It is I who am honored by the queen's attention. Everyone will envy me because the queen has deigned to notice me."

Then Mr. Neufeld would applaud. "Bravo, Gertie, bravo. Soon you'll be getting a telegram from Second Avenue: Bessie Thomashefsky is sick and they want you to go on in her place."

But he never applauded for Lilly. Poor Lilly. She was the best-looking girl in Brownsville, and she had recited "The Year's at the Spring" for Miss Katz in a voice that sounded like singing. No one could blame Miss Katz for having picked Lilly to be Queen Esther—no one except Berenice. But Lilly couldn't remember her lines. She just couldn't.

Mr. Neufeld tried to help. "Don't read it, Lilly. You've read it enough times. Put the paper down and try to say it."

Obediently, Lilly placed her script in her lap. "I want . . . I beg . . . I'm giving a party. Please come."

"Oh, no, Aunt Lilly," I sighed.

"That's what the line means, doesn't it?" Lilly protested. "So what difference does it make if I don't say it just like it's written there?"

"The way you say it doesn't sound right," I tried to explain. "Miss Katz will get mad if you don't say it the way it's written."

Lilly knew that what I said was true. Miss Katz had made up the play herself and she liked it the way it was. Besides, it was hard on the other actors if Lilly said her lines a different way each time.

"Listen to me, Aunt Lilly," I said. "Listen hard." I put down the script and recited slowly: " 'If it please the king to grant my request, let the king and Haman come to a banquet that I shall prepare for them, if I have found favor in the king's sight.' Now say that."

"If it please the king," Lilly began again, "the king . . . the king can come . . ."

"Listen again, Aunt Lilly," I interrupted, keeping my

93

voice as calm as I could. "Listen again."

But if she finally got a line right one night, by the next night she had forgotten it. She just couldn't make the words stick in her head. Mr. Neufeld and I worked so hard trying to help her we went to bed each night with headaches. After two weeks, he and I knew the entire play by heart. Lilly still didn't know her own speeches.

Each day as I came home from school I ran to check the mailbox. I thought maybe my father's birthday letter had somehow been delayed on its long trip east, but there was never a single thing for me in that box. There was hardly ever a letter for anyone, just the gas bill every month and a water bill twice a year. Mr. Goldfarb left his bill in the milkbox and the insurance man came each month in person for his two dollars. Heat from the coal furnace was included in the rent.

Once I did see an envelope in the box. I felt my throat close and my heart beat more quickly. It wasn't the middle of the month; this time it couldn't be the gas bill. But when I pulled the envelope out of the box with shaking fingers, I saw that it wasn't addressed to me. It was addressed to Mr. Neufeld. I took it upstairs and put it on the dresser in his room. I was allowed in his room because I cleaned it. When he came home,

I told him about the letter. It was postmarked "Chicago." I hoped he'd tell me what was in it, but when he came out of his room for dinner, he didn't say a word about it, not then, or afterward, when we were alone in the kitchen. I controlled myself and didn't ask, not outright, anyway. I just dropped a few casual remarks as I washed up.

"I put your letter on your dresser, Mr. Neufeld," I said.

He was reading the *Atlantic Monthly*. He looked up from the magazine and said, "Yes, Gertie, I know. Thank you."

"I check the mailbox every day," I explained. "There's hardly ever anything in it, but I'm always hoping for a letter from my father. I think my birthday letter was delayed. It's a long trip here from Colorado."

"Yes," Mr. Neufeld agreed. "A lot of things could happen to a letter between Colorado and New York."

"Even between Chicago and New York," I commented.

He smiled a little and nodded. Then his eyes dropped back to the *Atlantic Monthly*.

"But your letter made it all right."

He looked up again. He wasn't smiling. "Yes," he said sharply. "As you noticed from the postmark, it got here in five days." I knew from his tone I had gone far enough.

But in another moment he relented. He put down the magazine and spoke to me quietly. "I'm sorry the letter from your father hasn't come yet. How's your mother?"

I shrugged. "I don't know. We were there last month, and we won't go again until school's out, I guess. I don't really care. She's not going to get better."

"You can't be sure of that." he answered gently.

I felt myself grow hot with fury. "What's the good of hoping?" I said, my voice full of the bitterness I felt. "It's so unlikely. I try not to think about her."

"But you can remember her the way she was, before she got sick."

"She got sick on purpose, you know."

"What?" A puzzled frown creased his forehead.

I turned and looked at him directly. "That's what Grandma thinks. And I think she's right."

He nodded, as if he understood now. "So you're mad at her."

"Sure, I'm mad at Grandma a lot of times," I admitted. "Anyone can see that."

"No," Mr. Neufeld replied softly. "At your mother."

I didn't answer.

"And at your father too, for leaving."

Again, I said nothing.

"It's all right, you know," Mr. Neufeld went on, almost as if he were talking to himself. "It's all right to be angry at them. They did leave you, each in a different way. I believe they both love you very much, and they couldn't help leaving you. But they did go, and naturally that makes you angry. The important thing to remember is that it's really them you're angry at. Don't take it out on everybody else."

I felt myself flush with annoyance once again. "When was I fresh to you?" I asked.

"Never," he replied firmly. "You're always wonderful to me."

"I don't see why I have to be nice to the aunts. They treat me awful."

He answered me slowly. "You don't make it easy for them to treat you nicely."

"It's not my fault." I spit each word out with venom.

"Perhaps not." He closed his magazine and laid it on the floor beside the rocking chair in which he was sitting. "Would you like to work on some Hebrew now?"

"No," I said. "I'm tired. I'm going to bed." I tossed the dish towel over the faucet and stalked out of the kitchen. Actually, it was too early to go to bed, but I had told Mr. Neufeld that was where I was going, so that's where I went. It took me a long time to fall asleep, however, and I thought about a lot of things. Mr. Neufeld was right about one person, for sure, one person he didn't even know.

The next day, at recess, I stood by the fence and watched Ellen O'Grady walk back and forth across the playground with Sylvia Enders and Polly Flanagan, who had become her best friends since our fight. With all my mind, I willed Sylvia and Polly suddenly to feel a terrible need to rush off to the girls' room, leaving Ellen alone so that I could approach her. But it didn't work. Recess was nearly over. I realized I was going to have to do the task I'd set for myself the hard way.

The three turned around at the school's side wall and started back toward the fence. I met them halfway, in the middle of the playground. Sylvia and Polly were walking with arms linked. Ellen was next to Polly, her head turned to listen to what Polly was saying, but with a little space between the two of them.

"Ellen!" I said, loud and clear.

The three girls stopped. Ellen's face turned toward me, a dark look in her eyes. I spoke quickly. "Ellen, can I talk to you?" She turned her head away. "Please," I added. "Please."

She turned back toward me again. "All right," she said slowly, flatly.

"Alone." I made my voice as soft as I could, and then I added once again, "Please."

"Oh, I was going to the girls' room now anyway," Polly offered. Unlike Fanny Mercer, Polly didn't actually hate me.

"Me too," Sylvia said. The two of them walked off together, still arm in arm.

Ellen stared after them. When she faced me again there was a very slight smile on her lips. "They do everything together," she said. "Even going to the bathroom."

I didn't waste any time. "I'm sorry, Ellen," I said. "I'm sorry I got so mad at you that day. I had no reason to. You were just trying to help. You were just trying to make things better."

Ellen nodded slowly, her green eyes open wide.

"My mother's crazy," I said. "I know it."

"Sick," Ellen said.

"Sick and crazy."

"My father drinks," Ellen said. "Saturday nights he gets so drunk he falls down on the tavern floor and the barkeep has to send for my brothers to drag him home."

I nodded. I had known that. It was something everyone in the neighborhood knew, like my mother's being crazy.

The bell rang, signaling the end of recess. We walked back toward the building. "We can eat lunch tomorrow if you want," Ellen said.

"Won't Polly and Sylvia mind?" I asked hesitantly.

"They won't miss me," Ellen said. "But we could eat with them. They wouldn't mind that either."

"All right," I said. "Race you to the door." We started to run. I was taller, stronger, and faster than Ellen, but I let her beat me anyway.

SEVEN

As Purim drew closer, Lilly got quieter and quieter. The play was to be presented the Sunday before the holiday. The Brownsville Talmud Torah's Parents' Organization was charging only a dime to see it. They planned to make real money selling refreshments. Everyone predicted the hall would be jammed. Even if no one came but the mothers, fathers, sisters, brothers, grandmothers, grandfathers, aunts, uncles, and cousins of the people in the cast, the hall would be jammed.

Grandma and Berenice didn't know that Lilly still hadn't memorized her lines. Mr. Neufeld didn't say anything about it to anyone, not even to Lilly herself. I suppose Miss Katz was upset, but she must have thought it was too close to the performance to give the part to anyone else. Altogether, there had been only one month between the day of the tryouts and the day of the performance. The cast had rehearsed Sunday afternoons and two evenings each week. One night when she got back from rehearsal, Lilly told Mr. Neufeld and me that Miss Katz had appointed Mrs. Weissbinder prompter. Lilly seemed to relax a little after that.

On Sundays I went for rolls two hours later than on weekdays. The day of the performance, the Sunday before Purim, was damp and misty. I could smell spring coming. When I got home, Grandma had already put up the coffee, and that smelled good too. Berenice and Mr. Neufeld were sitting at the table, waiting for the rolls.

"Where's Lilly?" I asked after I'd eaten my own roll, spread thickly with the apple butter Grandma put up every fall.

"The queen is still getting her beauty sleep," Berenice said with a snort.

"You better go wake her," Grandma said. "She has a lot to do before the show."

"I thought she'd be too excited to sleep late this morning," I said as I left the kitchen. In our bedroom, Lilly lay in the cot, but her eyes weren't shut. They were staring at the ceiling.

"What's wrong?" I asked her.

"I don't feel well," she said.

"You have to feel well," I replied. "Today is the day. Today is the play." As if she didn't know.

Slowly Lilly turned her head toward me. "I can't do it," she said. "I can't be in the play. Go tell Miss Katz I'm sick. Go right now and tell her I have a fever of 104. Tell her I'm dying."

"But Aunt Lilly," I cried, "you can't do that. You can't disappoint everyone that way."

"Gertie, I can't make a fool of myself either. That'll be worse."

"Mrs. Weissbinder," I began, "the prompter—"

"She says the line, and then I say it. That's the dumbest thing of all." Lilly's voice was full of disgust.

"But they've sold all those tickets," I reminded her. "Morrie said yesterday they sold 143 tickets."

"Miss Katz can be Esther. That'll suit her just fine. Go tell her, Right now."

"Aunt Lilly, I can't," I protested.

"Go. Go right now." She sat up in bed. "If you don't

go, I'll give you such a slap your face will be red the rest of your life!"

I left the bedroom and went back into the kitchen. My coat was hanging on a hook by the kitchen door. "Where're you going?" Grandma asked as she saw me put it on. "You haven't done the breakfast dishes yet."

"I'll do them when I get back. I have to see Miss Katz. I have to tell her Lilly's sick and can't be in the play."

Grandma's mouth dropped open, but I hurried out of the room before she could ask any more questions. It was enough I had to explain to Miss Katz. Let Lilly take care of her own mother.

I was halfway down the block when Mr. Neufeld caught up with me. "I'll walk with you," he said. "Tell me what's going on."

I could tell him the truth because he knew about Lilly's problems with her lines already. "Lilly's scared she'll look like a fool on that stage this afternoon," I explained. "She told me to tell Miss Katz she's sick. She says Miss Katz can play the part herself."

Mr. Neufeld shook his head. "Miss Katz will never see thirty again," he said. "She'll make a fool of *herself* if she's Queen Esther to a sixteen-year-old King Ahasuerus." He had met Miss Katz when she'd dropped off the material for Lilly's dress.

"Yes," I agreed. Then I shut my mouth.

"Why not tell Miss Katz you'll be Queen Esther?" Mr. Neufeld put his hand on my shoulder. "You know all the lines."

It didn't surprise me to hear him say such a thing. The thought had occurred to me, but I hadn't dared to put it into words. "I don't know the movements," I said. "I never rehearsed it."

"It's only nine-thirty. The play doesn't go on until three. Miss Katz can tell you what to do in that time. You're very quick, Gertie. You'll remember what she tells you."

I stopped still on the sidewalk and so did he. "I can't say those things to Miss Katz," I whispered. "I can't. You come with me. You say them."

"I'll come with you," Mr. Neufeld agreed, "but I won't ask her to give you the part. You tell her you can do it, and then I'll back you up."

For a moment we stood there, staring at each other. Then I nodded my head. "All right," I said. We walked on in silence until we came to the apartment house on Eastern Parkway in which Miss Katz lived with her mother. It had a lobby with a tile floor, rubber plants, and a carpeted stairway. We walked up to the third level and knocked on the door of Apartment 3C. Mrs. Katz opened it up. When she heard we had come to see her daughter, she led us into the kitchen. Miss Katz, wearing a flowered kimono, was sitting at the table drinking coffee and reading *Vanity Fair* magazine.

"Good morning, Miss Katz," I said.

She looked up from her magazine. "Good morning." She frowned a little. "Do I know you?"

"I'm Gertie Warshefsky," I said. "I'm Lilly Grobowitz's niece." I began to talk very quickly. "You see, she's sick. She has a fever of 104. She can't get out of bed." Miss Katz's face blanched white, but I rushed right on. If I gave her the chance to say something, I might lose my nerve. "But I know her part. I know every word of it, and I know all the cues too. I can do it. And I'm tall for my age. I'll look all right. Would you like to hear me say some of the lines?"

Miss Katz was too startled to answer my question. Mr. Neufeld decided it was his turn. "Listen to her, Miss Katz," he said. "You won't be sorry."

Miss Katz's eyes darted from Mr. Neufeld to me. She opened her mouth as if she was going to say something, but I didn't wait. I took her movement as a signal to begin. I put on my Queen Esther voice. It was really my own voice at its best. "Let my life be given me at my petition," I said loud enough to rattle the dishes on the shelf. "For we are sold, I and my people, to be destroyed, to be slain, to perish." Then I fell to my knees and spoke in a kind of whisper, but still loud, "Have mercy, my lord. Have mercy on your queen who loves you, and on her people, who are innocent of any crime."

Miss Katz's eyes examined my face intently. "You're sure Lilly can't do it?" she asked.

"I'm sure. She has a fever of 104." The lie slipped through my lips so easily that I amazed myself.

An odd expression on her face, Miss Katz sighed. It sounded as if it might have been a sigh of relief. "All right," she said. "We have a lot of work to do. We'll get started immediately."

"But I have to go home," I said. "I have to clean up the breakfast dishes. I'll be back as soon as I can."

Mr. Neufeld laughed. "Never mind about that, Gertie," he said. "I'll go home. I'll tell your grandmother what's happened."

"She'll be mad."

"I don't think so. But if necessary *I'll* do the breakfast dishes." He came up to me and shook my hand.

"Good luck, Gertie. I'll see you at three o'clock this afternoon. We all will."

"Except Lilly," I reminded him hastily. "She's sick."

"Yes, of course. Except Lilly."

Miss Katz and I worked very hard for the next five hours. First she went over the play with me right there in her apartment. This time, I played Esther and she played all the other parts. I knew the lines perfectly. By the time we had run through them all, Miss Katz was smiling. She sent a neighbor's boy over to our flat to get Lilly's white Queen Esther dress, and she had her mother take in the bust and waist so it would fit me. She lent me her own kimono to wear in the opening scenes, before Esther gets to be queen.

After that we went over to the hall and I learned the movements on the platform. Miss Katz ran around like a cockroach, trying to be all the other people in the cast at once, at the same time that she was showing me where to stand and where to walk. About one-thirty, other kids started drifting in. Morrie, Mel, and Mildred Levy arrived together. Morrie took one look at Miss Katz and me prancing around on the platform and then he let out a yell from the back of the room. "Hey! What's going on here?"

"Lilly's sick," Miss Katz replied briskly. "Gertie here

was kind enough to offer to play the part. She knows the lines," she concluded significantly.

Morrie, Mel, and Mildred hurried down the center aisle. "I know the lines too," Mildred said. "You could have asked me to do it."

"Then I'd have to teach you Esther's part and Gertie, Vashti's," Miss Katz explained, a faint note of apology in her voice. "There wasn't enough time for all of that."

"So Lilly's sick," Mel said in his quiet way. "Poor Lilly."

"Poor Lilly, my foot," Mildred retorted. "You know perfectly well—"

"Lilly *is* sick," I interrupted. However mad I got at Lilly myself, I resented Mildred's innuendos. "She has a fever of 104."

Mildred snorted and raised her eyebrows. Morrie smiled a small, knowing smile. Mel leaped lightly onto the platform. "Good for you, Gertie," he said. "It's really swell of you to help out this way."

"Now that you're here," Miss Katz said, "I want all of you up on the stage. I want you to walk through the show very quickly to make sure Gertie knows where she's supposed to be."

"I have to get dressed," Mildred said.

"It will only take half an hour," Miss Katz answered sharply. "There's still plenty of time." She trotted down the steps and rounded up the cast members gathered in the auditorium, which by this time were nearly all of them.

"Are you scared, Gertie?" Mel whispered to me.

"I guess I would be if I'd had time to think about it," I told him with a little laugh, "but I've been too busy. Miss Katz and I haven't eaten lunch."

"Here." Mel reached in his jacket pocket, pulled out some licorice strings, and handed them to me. He was much better looking than Mr. Neufeld, but otherwise they had a lot in common.

After our quick run through the show, we dressed in the kitchen, where the ladies of the Brownsville Talmud Torah's Parents' Organization were making coffee and laying out piles of hamentashen on trays. I loved those three-cornered pastries stuffed with prune or poppy seed, which were prepared especially for Purim. The ladies offered us some, and I wanted one badly. The licorice hadn't made much of a dent in my hunger. But Miss Katz wouldn't let any of us take them. "After the performance," she said. "Not before. Before will make you thirsty, and your tongue will stick to the roof of your mouth."

Just ten minutes later I found myself, with the rest of the cast, standing behind one of the screens Miss Katz had placed on either side of the platform so we'd have a place to wait our turns without being seen. The other kids all poked their heads around the screens to see if they could find their friends in the audience.

"Oh, look . . . there's Uncle Izzy. I didn't know he was coming. . . ."

"If my mother doesn't get here soon, she won't find a place to sit down. . . ."

"They're making the little kids sit on the floor in the front. . . ."

"*Psst* . . . hey, Ike, give me a couple of your jelly beans."

But I didn't poke my head out. I didn't want to know who was there. Now that I had stopped moving, I was scared. Saul Kramer had pulled open the curtains. Morrie and Selig Gross were talking. I scarcely heard them. I felt as if there were a rock in the bottom of my stomach, and all I really wanted to do was go to the toilet. I was glad now that I hadn't eaten. I was sure that fact alone was saving me from throwing up.

But soon Mel pushed me out on the stage with a gentle shove. Morrie, dressed in a striped bathrobe with a Turkish towel wrapped around his head, said to me, "Cousin, the king has commanded that all the maidens in the kingdom appear before him so that he may choose a new queen."

I opened my mouth. Somehow the line I was supposed to speak squeaked itself out. "But cousin, I do not wish to appear before the king along with a thousand other maidens. I am not a sheep to be picked over at a market."

From out in front came a ripple of laughter, and suddenly I felt easier. "But you must," Morrie-Mordecai replied. "If you are chosen, it may be that you will have the opportunity to serve your people."

I answered Mordecai with my next line, and after that I forgot that I was on a stage, and I forgot all those people sitting out in the audience. Well, I didn't actually forget them; it's just that they weren't on the top of my mind any more. What was on the top of my mind was the fact that I was Queen Esther. I was the most beautiful woman in all of Persia, and the king, who was Mel and Ahasuerus all at the same time, chose me for his bride. He chose me even though I wouldn't put on perfumes and makeup and gorgeous clothes, like all the other candidates. Of course, he didn't know that I was a Jew, but, as later events were to prove, his knowing wouldn't have made any difference.

What had taken so many hours to learn went by as quickly as a dream when we did it in front of an audience, without interruptions, except for laughter and applause. I did make a few mistakes, but so did some of the others. There was one point at which Mordecai overhears some men plotting to kill the king, and warns the king's guard. The men are put to death, but the king doesn't know anything about the affair until weeks later when his scribe reads the whole story to him out of a book. Then the king calls in Haman and asks him how to reward a man the king wishes to honor. Naturally, Haman thinks the king is talking about Haman himself, and when he finds out it's Mordecai who's to be led through town on the king's own horse by a nobleman who sings his praises, Haman is furious, especially as the king makes Haman do the honoring. It's after that that Haman vows to get revenge by having all the Jews in Persia killed. Selig skipped a whole speech in that scene but Flo Greenfield, who played his wife, covered for him very well, and no one in the audience knew. No one in the audience knew about any of the other mistakes either. They thought the production was perfect.

We came to Esther's important moments. Morrie-Mordecai told me I must appear before the king even at the risk of my life. I prayed to God for his help. I realized that I had to do as Mordecai had told me. I had to let the king know that I was one of the despised people Haman wished to destroy, that I was a Jew.

Bowing low, I approached the throne of the king.

"What do you want?" Mel asked. His own voice was deep enough to be Ahasuerus' without his changing it. "For whatever you ask for, even if it is half my kingdom, I will give it to you."

Now came the lines that Lilly had never been able to make any sense out of at all. I wanted to seem dignified and nervous at the same time, so I stood very straight and clenched my fists. "If it please the king to grant my request, let the king and Haman come to a banquet that I shall prepare for them, if I have found favor in the king's sight."

At the banquet I sang a song. I held Miss Katz's ukulele in my hand and pretended to play it while I sang. Actually it was Miss Katz who was doing the playing, on another ukulele, behind the screen. That song was the one thing Lilly would have done better than I. Her voice was really pretty; mine was only passable. But they heard me. They all heard me.

After my song, Mel and Selig applauded. So did everyone in the audience. And then Mel said, "Whatever you want, Queen Esther, it will be granted. Even if it is half my kingdom, I shall give it to you."

I fell on my knees before the king. "Have mercy, my lord," I cried. "Have mercy on your queen, who loves you, and on all her people, who are innocent of any crime." I felt tears fill my eyes as I spoke.

The king looked at me in surprise. "But who is it that wishes to destroy you, or your people? You are the queen. Who would dare?"

I stood up then, pulled myself to my full height, and pointed my finger at Selig-Haman. "HIM!" I shouted in my loudest voice. "HIM!" And then I turned to the king and said in a softer voice, but a voice full of pride, "My lord, I am a Jew!" When I said that, I heard someone in the audience start to applaud. Later I thought it must have been Mr. Neufeld. Others out front began to clap too, and pretty soon the whole room was applauding.

Then the king told me he couldn't cancel the order to kill the Jews that Haman had tricked him into issuing, because it bore the king's seal. But the Jews could fight back when Haman's army attacked them. So after the banquet came the big battle scene, with Morrie as Mordecai joyfully brandishing a cardboard sword as leader of the troops. When at last the Jews were victorious, I, Esther, stood up and faced the audience. "Ever since that fateful day," I announced, "we Jews have marked the anniversary of our deliverance from the hands of the wicked Haman. On the fourteenth day of Adar we remember Mordecai and Esther with a joyful celebration. What is the name of that celebration?" I asked.

"Purim!" several voices in the audience called out. "Purim."

"Purim," I repeated. "Happy Purim to all of you."

"Happy Purim," the audience shouted back at us. "Happy Purim." Then they started to applaud. Mel, Selig, and Morrie stepped forward to stand on a line with me. Mel took one of my hands, Morrie took the other, and we all bowed low. Saul Kramer pulled the curtain shut. The Brownsville Talmud Torah's Purimspiel was over.

Afterward, still wearing our costumes, we drank coffee, tea, and little cups of sweet wine, and ate hamantashen. Everyone crowded around me, smiling at me, touching me.

"You were wonderful, Gertie. . . ."

"What a queen. A natural. Born to it. . . ."

"I could hear every word you said. All the way in the back I could hear you. . . ."

Mr. Neufeld shook my hand. Grandma kissed me. So did Miss Katz. "Gertie saved the day," she said. "Did you all know that Gertie saved the day?"

Even Berenice spoke to me. "You were good," she said. "You were a lot better than Lilly would have been. I didn't know you had it in you." I kissed Berenice. I wanted to kiss everyone in the room. If Lilly had been there, I would have kissed her too. I felt as if I were floating.

But after a while everyone went home. I had to change into my skirt, middy and black stockings. I had to give the kimono and the white gown back to Miss Katz. "Hurry up, Gertie," Berenice called to me while I was dressing in the kitchen. "We can't wait all day for you, you know."

I walked back home with Grandma, Berenice, and Mr. Neufeld. It was getting dark, and the weather had turned cold again. A light, icy rain was falling. It pricked my face like needles.

When we got into our apartment, I went into the bedroom to see Lilly. Her eyes were shut. I couldn't tell if she was really asleep or not, but I knew she didn't want to hear about what had happened. Grandma called me to set the table for supper. We ate our potato soup and our bread and margarine and drank our tea. By then the icy rain had turned to sleet, and I could hear it slicing at the windowpanes.

We were in the middle of our supper when Lilly came out of the bedroom and joined us at the table. We had been talking about the play, but we stopped as soon as she walked into the kitchen. Because Grandma, Mr. Neufeld, and even Berenice were afraid of hurting Lilly's feelings, I realized there would never be much conversation about the play in our house. I wouldn't have the opportunity of living that wonderful afternoon over and over again by talking about it with the family. And I couldn't talk about it at school. No one in my class had seen it. They wouldn't understand. They'd only be bored or think I was bragging, except maybe Ellen, and I wasn't even sure about her.

"How do you feel?" Grandma asked Lilly.

"All right, I guess," Lilly replied.

Grandma put her hand on Lilly's forehead. "No more fever," she said. "You never did feel very warm to me. But you better stay home from school tomorrow anyway." She turned to me. "Get Lilly some soup," she ordered.

Lilly waved her hand. "I don't want any soup. Just a cup of tea." The pot was in front of Mr. Neufeld. He poured for her. She added sugar and milk and took a deep, long sip. She put her cup down and looked at Berenice. "I'm sorry, Berenice," she said. "I don't think any more that you pushed me out of the bed on purpose. I'm sure you didn't."

Berenice grunted.

"I'd like to come back into the bed now," Lilly said. "The cot's very uncomfortable."

"It's your bed as much as mine," Berenice said. "Suit yourself."

"The cot *is* uncomfortable," I complained. "Why must I always be the one to sleep in it?"

Grandma turned her sternest face to me. "You want I should put up a sign?" she asked.

"No," I sighed. I really didn't want to hear all over again about my parents' uselessness and my grandmother's generosity in providing a home for an undeserving orphan. "I'll go back to the cot." They were all so worried about Lilly's feelings. Why didn't anyone think of my feelings, at least on that day, of all days? "But you better switch the linen," I added. "I don't want to catch whatever Lilly's got."

Lilly and Berenice went off to do as I'd asked without argument. Grandma went upstairs to discuss the day's events with Mrs. Augustine. I carried the dishes over to the sink. I turned on the faucet and watched water run into the dishpan. Water was running down my cheeks too. I hadn't meant to cry, but I couldn't help myself. The tears came without my permission, and so did a sob or two.

Mr. Neufeld looked up from his book. "What's the matter, Gertie?" he asked, his voice gentle.

I turned and faced him. "Nothing has changed," I spit out the words. "Everything is just the same. It all lasted such a little time."

Mr. Neufeld got up out of his chair and came over to me. He put his arm around my shoulder. "Try not to feel too bad about that, Gertie," he said. "You were queen for a day. Some people don't have even that, ever, in their whole lives."

"But it's not enough," I shouted. I was angrier than I'd ever been. "Queen for a day is not enough."

"Well," Mr. Neufeld explained, his voice soothing me, "it wasn't actually just for a day. Underneath, the real you is always a queen. I know it, and you know it, and some other people suspect."

I couldn't help smiling a little, even as I shook my head disbelievingly.

"You see," Mr. Neufeld went on, "you're the one who knows who you really are. Other people can only guess, and lots of times they make mistakes—just as lots of times you make mistakes about other people."

"I do?" I thought about Ellen. "Yes, I do."

"You're a brave girl, Gertie, and you're a smart one. Your chance to show everyone that you're really a queen will come again, and when it does, you'll have the eyes to see it and the nerve to take it. Won't you Gertie?"

"I don't know." I wasn't over being angry. "It isn't fair."

Mr. Neufeld looked right into my eyes. He spoke very slowly. "Promise me, Gertie," he said. "Promise me that you'll watch for your chance, and that when it comes, you'll take it. You'll remember Queen Esther, and you'll take your chance when it comes."

I didn't really know what he meant. But I could tell he was very serious. "I promise," I said. "I'll remember Queen Esther all my life. You can be sure of that."

"Some day, some other day, the queen inside you

will come out again," Mr. Neufeld said. "I know it."

I wiped my cheek with the dish towel. "Thanks, Mr. Neufeld."

He reached into his jacket pocket and pulled out a chocolate bar. "How about a little dessert?" he asked.

"We'll share it," I said.

He broke the bar in half and handed one of the pieces to me. He lifted the other piece high in the air. "To Gertie," he said. "A cheer for Queen Gertie. Hip, hip, hooray. Hip, hip, hooray."

I laughed and shook my head. "Mr. Neufeld," I said, "I don't know what I'm going to do with you." Then I popped my chocolate into my mouth. There was always the chance that Berenice or Lilly might come into the kitchen unexpectedly and insist on a piece. It was my chocolate, mine and Mr. Neufeld's. They weren't to have a single bite.

EIGHT

Aunt Lilly and Aunt Berenice got candy from Mr. Neufeld anyway. So did Grandma.

The holiday of Purim came. For me its true celebration had occurred not in the synagogue, but three days earlier, in the Brownsville Talmud Torah. One night, nearly a week later, I was still feeling kind of let down and sorry for myself. As soon as we had finished dinner, Mr. Neufeld went into his room and brought out a huge five-pound box of chocolates, which he placed in the middle of the kitchen table. "For you ladies," he said. "For all of you."

Berenice didn't bother to say thank you. She just grabbed two pieces and stuffed them both in her mouth at once. Lilly, who had completely recovered both her health and her spirits now that the play was safely in the past, smiled and dimpled, said a musical "How kind of you, Mr. Neufeld," daintly selected a creme, placed it on her tongue, and sucked it slowly.

Mr. Neufeld chose a caramel. I picked an almond and Grandma ate a fruit. It was only after she had swallowed it that Grandma said, "Thank you, Mr. Neufeld. What's the occasion?"

Mr. Neufeld carefully rolled up his napkin and put it in his napkin ring as he spoke. "I have some news," he said. "I don't know whether you will regard it as bad news or good news. I myself feel disappointed about it, but I can't help it. The situation in Chicago is too good. I have to leave."

So that's what the letter postmarked "Chicago" had been about—some kind of job offer. Mr. Neufeld was leaving. He was leaving me. I felt like screaming—but of course I didn't. I just took another piece of candy from the box on the table.

"That's very bad news," Grandma said immediately. "You've been a wonderful tenant. I don't know where

I'll find another as good. I'm glad you have a chance to improve yourself," she added politely, "but I always thought you had a very good job."

"This is a chance to get into a business of my own, with my cousin," Mr. Neufeld explained. "He has a jewelry store, and his partner just died. He's looking for someone else and he thought of me. It's the ideal opportunity for me."

"But Mr. Neufeld . . ." I tried to keep my voice calm and reasonable. "You don't have a family. You make enough money for yourself. Why should you leave a good job for a situation you really don't know anything about?"

I was sitting next to him. He turned to me and put his hand on my shoulder. "Don't think I haven't gone over all of this in my mind a hundred times. I didn't say a thing about it before because I wasn't at all sure I was going to accept the offer. I have no family, and I've come to feel that this family is mine." His hand squeezed my shoulder, as if he were saying, "Especially you, Gertie." Then he went on. "But I don't like working hard for a business that isn't my own. To tell the truth, I'm tired of making money for men who aren't half as smart as I am. Remember what I told you after the play?"

I nodded slowly. "About taking your chance when it comes?"

"Yes," Mr. Neufeld replied, looking right into my eyes. "I have to do that too. It always costs you something, you know. Your never get your chance for nothing."

"And you think it's worth it?" I asked. "You think it's worth leaving us?" I really meant leaving *me*.

Mr. Neufeld turned up his palms and shrugged a little. His short-sighted brown eyes grew large behind his gold-rimmed glasses.

I pushed myself away from the table and, without saying another word, I left the kitchen. The conversation continued without me. I stopped in the front room for a minute and leaned against the wall, listening to what Grandma had to say. "When are you leaving, Mr. Neufeld?" she asked.

"I'm sorry, Mrs. Grobowitz, but I must go tomorrow," I heard him reply. "I'm taking the evening train from Grand Central."

"Tomorrow?" Grandma echoed him, dismay in her voice. "Tomorrow?"

"My cousin is desperate," Mr. Neufeld explained. "I delayed two weeks in telling him my decision, and now he can't wait any longer. If he doesn't have my help, he'll have to get someone else. But I'll leave you two weeks rent in lieu of notice. That's only fair."

I heard Grandma sigh with relief. With luck, she wouldn't lose a day's rent. This was the first time a tenant had been so generous. "So, Mr. Neufeld, you know we wish you all the best. We hope you'll keep in touch."

All Grandma really cared about was the money. I didn't stay to hear any more. I marched into the bedroom, slammed the door shut, and stayed there until Grandma called me to do the dishes. By that time Mr. Neufeld had gone into his room to pack. I hurried through my work as quickly as I could so that I'd be out of the kitchen before he came into it again. I sat on my cot to do my homework, and then I read until Berenice shut out the light.

The next afternoon at about four o'clock I was in the yard taking some laundry off the line when I glimpsed Mr. Neufeld down at the corner. He was coming back to pick up the bags he'd packed the night before. Then, according to Grandma, he was planning to rush off to Manhattan to catch his Chicago train. As soon as I saw him, I tore the last couple of things off the line as fast as I could and dashed into the building and up to our flat. I dropped the laundry basket in the middle of the kitchen floor, ran into the bathroom, and locked the door behind me.

I heard Mr. Neufeld come into the apartment and go to his room. I heard him come out again, his footsteps slower now because he was carrying two heavy bags and his basket. Most of his books he'd packed into cartons and sent off by mail, but if I knew him at all, I knew he'd be carrying some of his favorites with him—his big black Hebrew Bible and his Shakespeare, bound in red leather, and a couple of volumes of Graetz's *History of the Jews*. While he had been in his room Grandma had come into the kitchen to start dinner, and I now heard him speak to her. "Well, Mrs. Grobowitz, I'm afraid the time has come to say goodbye."

"Berenice and Lilly aren't home yet," Grandma said. "They told me this morning to say goodbye to you for them."

"Thank you," Mr. Neufeld replied. "Please say goodbye to them for me too, and tell them how much I enjoyed making their acquaintance."

"I'll get Gertie," Grandma offered. "You can say goodbye to her in person."

"Thank you," he agreed. "I certainly wouldn't want

to leave without making a proper farewell to Gertie."

"Not a chance," I thought to myself, trying to keep even my breathing very still.

Grandma's footsteps hurried out of the kitchen. She was going to look for me in the bedroom. She thought that's where I was. A few seconds later she was back. "Oi, that Gertie, she's never where you want her to be," she complained. "I know I heard her come in with the laundry, and I know I didn't hear her go out again. I was straightening your room and I heard her come in, I'm sure of it."

"I can't leave without saying goodbye to Gertie," Mr. Neufeld said in a worried tone. He raised his voice. "Gertie, Gertie, where are you?" he called. I remained absolutely quiet.

But some parts of me Grandma knew better than Mr. Neufeld did. I heard her footsteps click across the linoleum floor toward the bathroom. She turned the doorknob and pushed on the door. Of course, the door didn't open, because I had locked it.

"Are you done, Gertie?" she asked.

I didn't answer her.

"Are you done?" she repeated. "You've been in there long enough. There are other people in this house who have to use the toilet."

I knew I'd have to come out and face her eventually, so I decided I'd better reply. "I'm not done," I lied. "I have cramps."

"Mr. Neufeld has to leave. He has a train to catch. He wants to say goodbye."

"I can't come out. I can't."

Then I heard Mr. Neufeld's footsteps cross the linoleum floor. They too stopped at the bathroom door. "Goodbye, Gertie," he called. "I'll miss you, and I'll write to you."

I didn't say anything.

"Gertie!" Grandma's voice scolded.

" 'Bye," I mumbled.

I guess he heard me. If he didn't, I guess he understood anyway. "Goodbye, Gertie," he said again, and then, "Goodbye, Mrs. Grobowitz." More footsteps, more goodbyes, and then I heard the door slam. Seated on the toilet, I waited ten long minutes before I came out of the bathroom.

Not for a second did I think he'd write. If my father hadn't written in more than six months, why should a man who was no relation to me at all write?

I didn't have much to say the rest of that day, which didn't bother Grandma or the aunts very much. They only noticed when I talked what they considered too much, not when I talked less than usual. But the next day, at school, Ellen was not pleased with me. We were eating lunch on the front steps, she was chattering on about Fanny Mercer's birthday party, to which, naturally, I had not been invited, and I was saying nothing at all, not even "Really?" and "How nice."

Suddenly she punched my arm, announcing sharply, "Gertie! Gertie!"

I turned and looked at her. "What are you punching me for, Ellen?"

"I want to make sure you're awake."

"Of course I'm awake." I turned away again, annoyed that I had to answer her, annoyed at being shaken out of my thoughts.

"Why are you so cross?"

"I'm not cross," I snapped. "You're silly."

"If that's not cross," Ellen replied in an aggrieved tone, "I'd like to know what is."

After all the trouble I'd taken and embarrassment I'd suffered to make up with Ellen, I wasn't going to be so stupid as to have another fight with her. So I sighed deeply and told her what the matter was. "My friend left," I said. "You know, Grandma's boarder, Mr. Neufeld."

Ellen nodded. "I remember. You told me about him.

The one who was teaching you Hebrew. I'm sorry he's gone. But an old man like that can't really be your friend. You've still got me."

Ellen didn't understand. But in one way I supposed she was right. If he'd really been my friend, would he have left?

I managed to squeeze out a smile for Ellen. "Let's talk about something else," I said. "Tell me more about the party. Did they give favors?"

"We played Post Office," Ellen said. A kind of dreaminess came into her eyes. "I kissed Danny Connolly for a hundred and twenty-two seconds."

"Danny Connolly? Ugh!"

"It wasn't so bad," Ellen said. "It wasn't bad at all."

I was surprised to hear her say that. The only boy I could imagine not minding kissing was Mel Riesman, and I hadn't even seen him since the Purim play. He didn't come by anymore with Morrie. He was sort of involved with Mildred Levy. At least that's what Lilly said, but maybe she said it just to annoy Berenice. Actually, Berenice wasn't upset by Mel and Mildred. Mel had never meant anything to her anyway. Maybe Lilly said what she said about Mel and Mildred just to annoy *me*. Maybe she'd guessed how I felt.

"You like Danny Connolly," I stated flatly.

Ellen blushed and nodded. "Friday night I was sitting out on the stoop. He stopped and talked to me." Then her hand touched mine. "That has nothing to do with us, though. You know that."

I didn't know that. I didn't know that at all. But some things you can't help. Grandma always said nothing's sure but death and taxes. She was wrong. There's one more sure thing, if you just live long enough, and that's boys and girls.

I walked home very slowly after school that day. It was the first really fine day so far that spring. I should have been feeling the warmth of the sun on my back and looking at the crocuses in front of the private houses near Lincoln Park. Or I should have been hurrying home so that I'd be able to finish my work before it was too late to enjoy the evening. But I did neither of those things. Instead, I scuffed along, dragging the toes of my shoes across the sidewalk, watching my feet as I did it. I felt as if I were wrapped in a thick black cloud. I saw a big ant and a couple of smaller ones scurrying across the sidewalk, and I stepped on them. I threw a stone at two robins searching for worms on a front lawn, even though they were the first robins I'd seen that year. An early daffodil was blooming by a fence, and I snatched off its head and threw it in the gutter. If I could have snatched off my own head and thrown it in the gutter too, I think I would have.

When I got to our building, I lifted up my head and glanced automatically in the direction of the mailboxes alongside the front door. I had long ago given up expecting anything, but I looked there every day out of habit. And this time, there was a long white envelope in the box. It was much larger than the envelope the gas bill came in.

I dashed up the cement stairs and opened the box. I pulled out the envelope with such haste that I dropped it on the steps and had to bend over to pick it up. But it wasn't addressed to me. It was addressed to "Mrs. Lena Grobowitz." I turned the envelope over and looked at the return address printed on the back. "Broadmere State Hospital for the Incurably Insane." I read the last words again: INCURABLY INSANE. Up until that moment I had thought of the place where my mother lived simply as Broadmere State Hospital. I hadn't heard of the "incurably insane" part.

Then I did a terrible thing—truly, a wicked thing. I opened the letter. Even though it was addressed to my grandmother, I opened it. "It has to be about my mother," I told myself, "so it's all right if I open it. I'm entitled to know what it says. She's *my* mother."

But my fingers shook as I ripped the flap.

I read the letter. It was printed. They must have sent a letter just like it to the relatives of every patient in the hospital. It asked the family to send a nightdress, three sets of underthings, three pairs of stockings, and a pair of felt slippers for the patient's use in the ensuing year. If the family didn't want to send clothes, the letter said, they could send five dollars instead and the hospital would provide what was necessary.

I was properly punished. The letter hadn't been worth opening, and now I was going to have to find a way of explaining to Grandma how I had come to read it. I walked upstairs very slowly, thinking. Every explanation my imagination quickly seized upon was just as quickly rejected by the more sensible part of my brain. But when I let myself into the apartment, I found that Grandma wasn't home. She'd left a note on the kitchen table for me and the aunts. Actually, the note had been written by Mrs. Augustine. It said that Grandma and Mrs. Augustine had gone shopping for a dress for Mrs. Augustine to wear to her niece's wedding. The note had a P.S. just for me: "Gertie, peel the potatoes for supper before you start the ironing."

I didn't peel the potatoes and I didn't start the ironing. I still had the quarter Mr. Neufeld had given me for my birthday almost two months before. It was hidden on my shelf, beneath my long underwear. I got it from the bedroom and slipped it into my pocket. Then I took a paper bag from the kitchen cabinet. I took a nightgown and a set of underwear out of Grandma's drawer. She and my mother were about the same size, or had been, before my mother got so thin. I took Grandma's new house slippers out of the closet. I put the clothes and the slippers in the paper bag. I was stealing. Grandma would never forgive me, but I had already opened her mail and I thought it didn't matter much what else I did. Grandma always said a person might as well be hung for a sheep as for a lamb.

I walked to the subway station and embarked upon the long journey to Broadmere State Hospital for the Incurably Insane. I had taken a book with me to read on the train. I didn't want to think too much during the ride. Miss Needham had lent me this book too. It was *The Call of the Wild* by Jack London, and though I didn't like it as much as I had liked *Daddy Long Legs*, being fonder of orphan girls than of husky dogs, it was a good book and kept my mind occupied through the entire trip.

There was no one in the lobby of the building where

my mother lived. It was late in the afternoon and it wasn't a visitors' day. I just walked up the stairs and into the day room on her floor. No one stopped me. No one even said anything to me until I pushed open the door of the day room. But as soon as I crossed the threshold, one of the attendants was on top of me. I recognized her. She was the same one who had scolded my mother when I had visited with my grandmother on my birthday. She didn't remember who I was. "What are you doing here?" she asked in her sharp, angry voice. "No visitors today."

I held up the paper bag I was carrying. "I brought the things for my mother. The things they asked for in the letter."

"Who's your mother?" Her tone didn't soften one bit. She didn't feel sorry for me because my mother was incurably insane. But then, who did, except maybe Ellen, who was too busy now with Danny Connolly to care about me, and Mr. Neufeld, who was gone?

"Miriam Warshefsky," I replied.

"I'll see that she gets the things. You'll have to go now. It's time for our supper." She reached for my bag.

Quickly I put it behind my back. "It's too early for supper," I said. "I don't think it's even five o'clock yet."

"Five is when we have our supper," the woman said.

"This isn't a resort hotel, you know, though some of our inmates' families seem to think it ought to be."

"I'll give it to my mother myself," I said. "It'll only take a minute."

"That's impossible," the woman began. But while she had been talking to me, I had been looking around the big room and I had already glimpsed my mother sitting in a chair near a window. Before the attendant realized what I was doing, I slipped around her and hurried across the floor toward my mother. I was a fast runner. The attendant was much older than I, and much, much fatter. Though she came after me, I reached my mother before she could catch me.

"Hello, Mama," I said as I stood in front of her. Though my heart was beating so fast I could feel every thump, I spoke quietly. I didn't want to surprise or frighten her.

"If you don't leave right this minute, I will have to call a guard," the attendant said.

I didn't answer her. "It's me, Mama," I said. "It's me, Gertie."

My mother looked much the same as she had the last time I'd seen her. I was not startled by her appearance as I had been then. As I spoke to her, she tried to stand up, but she couldn't. A blue cord around her waist tied her to the chair.

I wheeled on the attendant. "Why did you tie her up like that?" I accused. "She's not a criminal."

"No, she isn't," the woman replied defensively, though in a much more subdued tone of voice. "But she *is* a baby. If she's not tied, she wanders all over the place—to the other floors, out into the yard. We don't have enough help around here to supply her with her own nursemaid. If you don't want her tied, she has to go to a locked floor. Or else you can send her to a private hospital," she added with a sneer. She knew perfectly well we couldn't afford anything like that.

Again I did not reply. I knelt beside my mother and took the felt slippers out of the paper bag. "Look what I brought you, Mama," I said. "Aren't they pretty?" I put them in her lap.

She smiled and stroked them. "Pretty," she said. "Pretty." She wiggled her feet out of her old slippers and handed me the new ones. I understood what she wanted. I leaned over and placed the new slippers on her feet.

The attendant had left me. I assumed that she was

going for one of the guards. I knew I didn't have much time. "I brought you a nightgown too," I said. I removed it from the bag as well and placed it in her hands.

"Pretty," she repeated, stroking the soft, worn flannel. "Pretty." Then she looked at me. "Thank you, pretty girl," she said solemnly. "Mimi darling loves you."

I stared at her. Mimi? Who was the Mimi that loved me? I didn't know anyone named Mimi. What on earth was she talking about? "Mimi?" I said it out loud. "Mimi? Who's Mimi?"

She giggled, a little three-year-old's giggle. With her right hand she struck her chest several times. "Mimi," she crowed. "Mimi. Mimi darling loves you."

Now I understood. Mimi was herself. "Mimi?" I asked again. "Is that what your mother calls you?"

She nodded. "Mimi knows. You're a good girl. A pretty girl. Mimi loves you."

"And I love you too, Mimi," I said. I had never known before that when my mother was little, Grandma had called her "Mimi darling." I stood up, leaned toward her, and kissed her on the cheek. Her skin was as soft as the old chamois Grandma used to polish the brass candlesticks.

The attendant was back. A man in a blue uniform walked next to her. She pointed an accusing finger in my direction. "There she is," she said. "Get her out of here."

"I'm going," I said. "I'm going right now. I just wanted to give my mother her things." I took the underwear out of the bag and laid it in her lap on top of the nightgown.

The guard looked at the attendant and shrugged. "What are you so upset about?" he seemed to be saying.

"Well, go on, get out of here. Right now," the attendant said. I could tell she was more annoyed with me than ever. For a moment I feared that she might take her anger out on my mother. But then I realized there wasn't anything she could do to my mother. My mother lived in her own world. She was three years old, and no one could touch her.

"Goodbye, Mimi darling," I said.

"Bye bye," she replied, waving her hand. "Will the pretty girl come again?"

"Yes," I said. "Soon." I turned and walked toward the door. The attendant walked alongside me, as if she were afraid I might change my mind. The guard was behind us. "I'm sorry if I disturbed your routine," I said. "I'm glad to see my mother looks no worse than she did last time."

"She's in good health," the woman replied grudgingly. "You don't have to worry about that. I watch them."

"If you could just take the rope off her . . ." I suggested softly.

She nodded. "Some days I can, when she's quiet."

"Thank you," I replied. "I won't come off hours again. I thought maybe, from the letter, she didn't have anything to wear."

"It's just a form letter."

I didn't tell her I already knew that. I said only, "Thank you," once again, and then I left. When I grew up and went to work, I'd tip the attendants. Then I could be sure they'd take good care of my mother. Until then, all I could do was be nice to them and come as often as I could, to make sure things were no worse than they had to be.

All the way home my mind was busy thinking about the good job I'd have when I was grown up, teaching school like Miss Katz or Miss Nedham, and earning twenty-five dollars a week so that I could buy my mother pretty wrappers and even ribbons for her hair. It was dark by the time I reached our building. It wasn't until I was climbing the stairs that I remembered my grandmother and the explanations I owed her, and the punishments I could expect. But I wasn't really sorry. I was glad I had gone to see my mother all by myself.

When I walked into the kitchen, I found my grandmother seated at the table. Berenice and Lilly were both there too, and even Mrs. Augustine, seated in Mr. Neufeld's rocker. As soon as she saw me, Grandma stood up, her hands clenching the edge of the table. "Gertie!" she cried. "Thank God you're here."

"What's the matter?" I asked. I couldn't imagine what was wrong. I thought something terrible had happened. "Why do you all look so worried?"

"For heaven's sake, you idiot!" Lilly scolded. "It's you. We've been worried sick about you. Where in the world have you been?"

"We were just about to send for the police," Berenice added. "Lilly was sure you'd been abducted by a white slaver. I just thought you'd fallen down a manhole."

"I knew you were all right," Mrs. Augustine chimed in, a broad smile turning her round cheeks into two red apples. " 'She's a big girl,' I told them, 'and she's a smart girl. She can take care of herself.' But they didn't listen. They went right on worrying."

For once in my life I was struck dumb. If I had done nothing all the way home but think about the various kinds of reactions I might encounter upon my arrival, I would never have thought of this reception. I'd never have thought of anything resembling a reception at all.

"Well, where were you?" Berenice asked. "We're waiting to hear."

Grandma turned on her. "Be quiet, Berenice. Gertie's worn out. Can't you see that? She hasn't had any supper. After she eats, she'll tell us all about it." She turned back to me. "Sit down, Gertie," she ordered.

In a daze, I obeyed. Grandma put a plate of potatoes and sour cream and a cup of steaming hot tea in front of me. I realized that I was as hungry as one of the dogs in Jack London's book. Four pairs of eyes stared at me as I gobbled the whole plateful up in no more than a minute and a half.

"Now, tell us," Berenice insisted as I swallowed the last morsel.

I shrugged. "It was nothing," I said. "I just went to see my mother."

Grandma reached her hand across the table and touched my arm. "You should have told us," she said. Her voice was quiet and firm, not loud or angry. "You should have left a note, like I did, so we wouldn't worry."

"I know, Grandma," I said. Suddenly I felt tears spring to the back of my eyes, and I blinked quickly. "I'm sorry. It was very bad of me. I'll never do a thing like that again."

"So, it doesn't matter now," Grandma replied gruffly. "All's well that ends well."

"There's something else," I murmured.

"What?" Grandma asked.

I stood up. "Let's go into the front room," I said.

Berenice and Lilly stood up too. "You stay here," Grandma instructed. She led the way out of the kitchen and I followed, shutting the door behind me. We sat down on the sofa that turned into Grandma's bed at night. I took the letter from the hospital out of my pocket and held it toward her.

"Read it to me," she said. She could have read it herself, but it would have taken her a long time. She'd never gone to school in English. She hadn't gone to school much in Yiddish either, to tell the truth.

I read it to her, and then I told her how I had taken her things. I blurted the whole story out as fast as I could. I wanted to get it over with. When it was done, she shook her head and frowned. "That was very, very bad of you, Gertie," she said. "I don't know which was worse, opening a letter with my name on it or stealing from my drawers. How could anyone as old as you act the way you have today?" Her voice was stern, but not really angry. She wasn't yelling, and I wasn't frightened.

"I know I was bad," I apologized. "I'm very, very sorry. I don't know what got into me."

Grandma's eyebrows shot up, as if to say that she knew. "So you'll have to be punished," she pointed out calmly. "That much you do know. You'll have to be punished."

I nodded slowly. What would the punishment be? What was the worst punishment she could give to me? She could make me quit school. And I'd have to do it, without an argument. I thought of asking her to make the punishment anything but that. Only I didn't. I felt I deserved the worst.

"You hate to iron," Grandma said. "For the next month, you'll have to do all the ironing in this house— every bit of it."

I couldn't believe what I had heard. I opened my mouth to say, "I do it all anyway," and then I shut it again, quickly, before the stupid words could tumble out. She already knew I did the ironing as well as I knew it. She wasn't punishing me. She wasn't punishing me at all. I opened my mouth again, and all I said was "Yes, Grandma."

"And no complaints," she added.

"No complaints," I promised.

Grandma stared at me for a long, silent moment, and I stared at her. I didn't know what she was thinking, and I was too worn out from all the day's surprises to do any more thinking myself. Then Grandma spoke. "It wasn't such a bad idea, bringing used things to your mother. She doesn't know the difference. And now I can spend the money I would have had to use on her for some nice material that Berenice can run up into spring skirts for herself and Lilly. For you too," she added, "if there's enough."

"You ought to spend the money on a new nightgown and slippers," I said, "to replace the ones I took."

"Slippers, maybe," she said. "I have a summer nightgown. Another flannel can wait 'til next fall." She stood up. "Nu, I better get those girls to clean up from supper. They'd never do it without being told."

I stood up too. "I'll do it," I said.

"No," she replied, "you just go to bed. Tomorrow's another day."

That was another one of Grandma's sayings. "Tomorrow is another day." I had never understood it. Of course tomorrow is another day. But that night I knew what it meant. It meant that tomorrow could be different.

NINE

Ellen didn't want me to go home after school the next day. She wanted me to hang around in the schoolyard with her, watching the boys play baseball. Actually, it was Danny Connolly she planned to watch, and not anyone else, but she wanted me with her. She didn't want her interest to appear too obvious.

"It's such a nice day," she added. "Who needs to be cooped up inside on an afternoon like this anyway?" She was right. It was a nice day, just as nice a day as yesterday had been.

"I'd like to stay, Ellen, really I would," I assured

her, "but I can't. I promised my grandmother."

"You're always helping," Ellen said. "Can't you skip one afternoon? What can she do to you anyway?"

"Maybe I could skip some other afternoon," I said, "but not this one. I was really bad yesterday, and I have to make up for it today."

"You were? You were *really bad?*" Ellen's voice sounded as if she couldn't imagine what really bad thing I could possibly do. "Tell me about it," she added eagerly.

"Oh, I will, Ellen, I will. Tomorrow. It's a long story, and I just don't have the time today."

Ellen didn't look very happy with that excuse, but, luckily for me, Danny Connolly came dashing down the steps at that very moment, bumping into Ellen accidentally on purpose.

"Oh, Danny," she squealed, "can't you watch where you're going?"

"Well, if you park yourself right in the middle of the sidewalk, you're just asking for it," he replied, a great grin spread over his round, freckled face.

"You hurt my arm," Ellen replied. She didn't sound as if the pain was exactly unbearable.

"I'll rub it for you," Danny offered, the grin, if possible, wider than ever. I didn't need to stay to hear any more of that conversation. I didn't dawdle on the way home either.

When I walked into the kitchen, Grandma was waiting for me. She was sitting at the table, peeling potatoes. A plate of cookies covered with a piece of waxed paper was on the table too.

"Hello, Grandma," I said as I dumped my books on the table. "I'll get to the ironing right away. Do you want me to finish the potatoes first?"

Grandma snorted. "What a change," she said. "I only hope it lasts." She pushed the cookie plate toward me. "First, eat something. I baked these oatmeal cookies this morning."

I was hungry. I was always hungry when I got home from school. I got the milk bottle out of the icebox, poured myself a glass, added a little coffee to it from the pot on the stove, sat down opposite Grandma, took a cookie, and bit into it. For a moment Grandma watched me chew, and then she said, very slowly, "Gertie, I have something . . . something surprising . . . to tell you."

I looked up at her, but I didn't say anything. I just kept on chewing.

"Mr. Neufeld gave me two weeks rent, to make up for leaving without notice."

I nodded. I had heard him say he was going to do that the night before he left. I didn't mention that it wasn't news to me. I couldn't understand why she was telling me about it anyway, or why she thought I'd find the information surprising.

She reached into her apron pocket and pulled out two envelopes. "These came today," she said. "I knew I'd better get to the mailbox before you did."

I blushed, but I didn't turn away. I was too curious to know whom the letters were from. Grandma's mailbox had never known so much activity in the year and a half that I had lived with her. "This letter came from Mr. Neufeld," she continued as she pulled a sheet of paper out of the envelope that had been torn open. The other she had laid face down on the table, and I could see that its flap was still sealed. "I couldn't imagine why Mr. Neufeld was writing to me. He knows I'm not from the readers, and he didn't owe me any money."

She paused as if she expected me to say something. "That is sort of queer," I agreed.

"It's a very short note," Grandma went on. "He printed it so it wasn't too hard to read. He says he's too busy getting organized to write much. He says he'll write a long letter to you as soon as he's settled." She shook the envelope briskly. "Do you know what's in here besides the note? You couldn't guess."

I didn't even try. I merely shrugged and bit into another cookie.

She extracted an oblong of thick paper from the envelope and waved it at me. "A money order," she said. "A postal money order for fifty dollars."

"But why?" I asked. "Why, if he didn't owe you anything?"

She shook her head slowly as she gazed at me. Just before I exploded with curiosity, she finally answered my question. "The note says the money is to help pay *your* keep!"

"My keep!" I exclaimed. "Mine?"

Grandma nodded. "Yes. Your keep. So I wouldn't make you leave school. He said he knew it wasn't enough, but he hoped it would help until your father gets back on his feet—as if he ever will. He said you were too smart to leave school."

My hand went to my mouth. I stared at my grandmother and shook my head, just as she had done a moment before.

"As if I didn't know that," Grandma said in a bemused, almost injured tone. "As if I didn't know that you're smart. As if I'd ever have made you quit."

"But Grandma," I cried, "you always said I should quit. You said it almost every day."

"Not lately," Grandma defended herself. "Anyway, I never meant it. I'd never break a law. If I did I'd be no better than your father, the deserter."

I was surprised to hear she knew children were supposed to stay in school until they were fourteen. I looked right in her eyes to see if she was telling the truth. I was only sorry that Berenice and Lilly weren't there, for witnesses. I didn't really think Grandma would go back on her word, though. One thing about her, she was perfectly honest. She never would have told me about the fifty dollars if she weren't.

But Grandma wasn't finished. "As if that wasn't enough surprise for one day," she said, "look at this." She picked up the other envelope and handed it to me. I recognized the writing immediately. The letter was from my father. "Like a voice from the dead," she added dryly. "Well, one thing we can be sure of, there's no money in *that* envelope."

I scarcely heard her, I was so busy tearing the flap. I pulled out the piece of paper inside. It was folded many times, and inside the folds, so as not to be noticeable through the envelope, there was a dollar bill. Silently I laid it on the table in front of Grandma. She pushed it back to me. "Keep it," she said. "It's not enough to make any difference. Use it to go to the Charlie Chaplin or the Keystone Kops with Lilly and Berenice next time."

I didn't waste a second picking up the dollar and putting it in my pocket. "Now read me the letter," Grandma ordered. "I could never make it out by myself. He writes like a chicken."

I didn't want to read the letter to her. It was my letter and I wanted to read it over slowly to myself when I was alone. But there was a look of firm expectancy on Grandma's face. I decided that this occasion was not one of the important ones on which I had to argue with her. I could let it go.

I cleared my throat and held the letter up in front of my face so she couldn't see it. "My darling Gertie," I began. "I am sorry I have not written you in such a long time. I guess I felt guilty, because things have not been going too well for me and I could not send you any money. But I received a letter last week from a friend of yours, Isaac Neufeld. He told me that it was very important that I write to you, even if I could not send any money. He said a letter from me without money was better than no letter at all. I cannot argue with that. From now on I will write to you every month, regardless, even if I am in jail (that's a joke)."

"Nu," Grandma humphed. "That may be his idea of a joke, but it isn't mine!"

I ignored her comment and went on. "It took a long time for Mr. Neufeld's letter to reach me. I am not in Denver any longer. I am in San Francisco. I am starting a new job tomorrow. I am only a clerk in a grocery store, but I have made up my mind to keep to business. This time I will make the most of my opportunities. In my next letter, I hope I will be able to send you more money." Luckily, I had been glancing ahead as I read and was able to skip saying the next few sentences out loud: "I know that will make things easier for you with your grandmother. She can be a regular old witch sometimes. No one knows that better than I. Still, she is taking care of you, and so you must try to be a good girl."

Grandma grew impatient with my silence as I read to myself. "Well, is that all?" she asked. "Does it end just like that? Doesn't he ask after your mother, or your aunts, or me?"

I read aloud again from "Try to be a good girl" and continued with, "Please write to me at the above address." Next I made up a line. "Give my regards to all the family," I said, and then went back to reading the words that were really on the page. "I think of you all the time. Your loving father, Benjamin D. Warshefsky."

"Well, go ahead, write to him," Grandma said. "You can use some of your dollar for paper and stamps. But don't expect to hear from him again next month, like he says. I've never in my life known him to keep his word."

"I had no idea Mr. Neufeld had written to him," I said. "I can't believe it."

"That Mr. Neufeld, he's deep," Grandma said, something other than approval in her voice. "Maybe it's just as well he's gone. A boarder isn't family. He doesn't need to know everything."

"What about the fifty dollars?" I asked.

"What do you mean, what about the fifty dollars?" she shot my question back at me. "I'll do with it just what he told me to do. It'll go toward your keep."

"What happens when the fifty dollars runs out?"

"I've been keeping you without any fifty dollars up until now, haven't I?" Grandma said, waving the potato she held in her hand in my direction. It was the fourth potato she'd peeled. It was my potato.

"And I can stay in school?" I wanted to make sure.

"I told you you could. How many times do I have to say it?"

"Twice is enough," I retorted. "Just don't forget."

"You don't have to get fresh," Grandma answered back. "I never forget. I never forget anything."

That was the truth. I was like her in that way. I didn't forget much either.

I picked up the envelope that Mr. Neufeld's money order had come in and turned it over. Sure enough, there was a return address on the back flap. I smiled to myself. As soon as I was done with the ironing, I'd take my dollar and go out. I'd buy paper and envelopes in the stationery store. Then I'd go to the post office and buy stamps—two stamps. At least two stamps. Maybe I'd buy more than two stamps. I might as well have them in the house. I might need them. In the future I might, after all, have quite a few letters to write!

ABOUT THE AUTHOR

BARBARA COHEN, perhaps best known for that little classic *The Carp in the Bathtub*, is also highly regarded for her novels, which include *Thank You, Jackie Robinson, Bitter Herbs and Honey*, and *The Innkeeper's Daughter*. She is also the author of *I Am Joseph* and *The Binding of Isaaac*, illustrated by Charles Mikolaycak. Mrs. Cohen lives in Somerville, New Jersey, with her husband Gene and their three daughters.

About *The Innkeeper's Daughter, School Library Journal* said: "A sensitive and satisfying semi-autobiographical novel of a young girl growing up in the late 1940's. . . . The mother-daughter relationship is well drawn; the era and place are nicely evoked, as is the supporting cast of characters."